AGENT OF TIME

A TIME TRAVEL ADVENTURE

NATHAN VAN COOPS

Grab an exclusive short story to accompany this book, absolutely free! Download your instant copy at nathanvancoops.com to join the race today!

PREVIOUSLY, IN TIMES LIKE THESE

This story takes place concurrently with the events of *In Times Like These* and relates to them directly.

If you have not read that novel, this story will contain spoilers.

If you would like a quick recap of the primary events of *In Times Like These*, you can find one at the end of this book via the table of contents.

I hope you enjoy the all new perspective on this multiverse of adventure.

-*Nathan*

1 / THE CRASH

December 30th-1985

Two Dead. Mysterious circumstances.

Special Agent Stella York scanned the photos of the deceased men, noting blank spaces where their names should be. It was a thin file. Even the dates of birth were missing, but one set of numbers had been neatly stamped next to each photo.

Date of death. December 29th, 1985.

Stella memorized the sparse details, then closed the file.

Special Agent Bartholomew MacGregor leaned across the armrest of the Ford Crown Victoria and aimed a knobby finger in her direction. "Remember your job is to keep your mouth shut and try not to make me look bad. The sooner we get through this, the sooner we get outta here. Got it?" Her new partner didn't wait for an answer, but rather turned and heaved his substantial body up and out of the car. He adjusted his sagging belt and moved toward the vehicle ahead of them.

Agent York sighed and checked her watch.

She had a theory that if Agent MacGregor could arrive anywhere on time for a change, he wouldn't be so ill-tempered when he got there. But they didn't seem in danger of finding that out anytime soon.

She climbed out of the car and straightened her jacket, then followed him across the street.

The white prisoner transfer van was still parked at the scene of the crash, though there was a tow truck standing by. Local PD had cordoned off the area and a couple officers with squad cars sat at the ends of the block redirecting traffic.

The front of the vehicle was caved in and there were scorch marks along the top and sides. No fire though. Stella thought the burns looked electrical. The rear doors had been closed, but otherwise the scene still matched the one described in the report. Minus the bodies.

A plain-clothes St. Petersburg police detective was waiting by the front of the vehicle and Special Agent MacGregor made straight for him, not bothering to study the scene. "Detective Briggs, I presume? Sorry we're late. Traffic was hell."

The handsome detective strode forward and extended a hand. "Special Agent MacGregor, I'm happy you were able to make it down. And this must be your partner." He turned his crystalline blue eyes to Stella as she walked up.

"Special Agent York is assisting," MacGregor replied.

The detective extended a hand to Agent York. "Danny Briggs. Nice to meet you." He had a pleasant, easy smile and damn good hair. It cascaded down the back of his neck in gravity-defying waves.

"We appreciate you keeping the crash scene intact till we could make it down," Stella said. "I know coordinating between agencies can have its delays."

"Glad we could get you down to the 'Sunshine City' for a bit."

"We certainly aren't complaining about the weather," Stella replied. "Must be ten degrees warmer than Jacksonville."

"It ain't a vacation," MacGregor grumbled. "What have we got?"

Stella frowned. Her partner hadn't always been so rude. When they'd first been assigned to one another, he'd even made attempts to be charming. But when she'd made it clear to him that simply being single and a woman didn't mean she had any intention of sleeping with him, he'd lost his pleasant demeanor. He seemed to be especially icy around guys that outclassed him in looks—which was basically all of them.

MacGregor addressed the detective again. "Anything new since yesterday?"

"Still no leads on the vehicle. Has New York government plates, as you know, so it looks to be an interstate transfer of some kind—that's no doubt why you got the call—but so far no one has a record of it. We've contacted all the prisons in the area. No one is reporting missing vehicles or inmates. Press got some pictures. Posted an article in the paper this morning calling it 'A Mystery Crash' on account of the van name." He pointed to the placard above the fender. "'GMC Savana.' We called a local dealership and they've never heard of it. Not a model they even make apparently. So there are a lot of things that don't add up."

"Like the registration sticker," Stella added, brushing a loose strand of hair behind her ear. "The date doesn't make sense."

The detective nodded. "That too."

Agent MacGregor frowned. "What's wrong with it?" He walked around the back of the van to view the license plate. The registration sticker listed the year as "10."

"That's either twenty-five years early, or maybe seventy-five years overdue," Detective Briggs said. "But I doubt they had registration stickers in 1910." He smiled.

"So we're dealing with amateurs," MacGregor said. "Some kind of custom van but they didn't have the sense to put a real name and sticker on it. That about it?"

"Could be," Detective Briggs replied. "But the oddities don't stop there." He walked to the front of the van. "We're calling it a crash because it obviously hit something, but we're not sure what."

"Would've thought that was obvious," MacGregor said. "Looks pretty well wrapped around that power pole to me." He ran a hand over the wrinkled hood.

Stella studied the scene. "True. But not this pole. It's not damaged."

Detective Briggs nodded. "Press didn't catch this tidbit, but unless we're dealing with some kind of miracle species of wood, there ought to have been a lot more evidence on the pole if it was hit this hard. There's not a scratch on it."

"I've seen stranger things," Agent MacGregor grunted as he peered into the driver's seat. "And no more news on the bodies?"

"Just what was in the report we sent over. Definitely homicides. Still waiting on the results of the fingerprint analysis. We've got somebody on that now, just waiting for a call. The bodies both showed evidence of electrocution. One was strangled and one was shot. Hard to say which happened first. Could be they were electrocuted after the fact. Coroner is still working on that."

"Electrocuted by what?" Agent York said, looking up at the power pole. The wires were still neatly suspended.

"Another good question," Detective Briggs replied. "Wish I knew. They told me to relay what we had and hand it off to you. We'll of course assist as much as possible."

Special Agent MacGregor marched around the van, peering into the windows, then backtracked and opened the rear doors. Unlike the driver's seat, there was no blood back here. MacGregor turned and elbowed Stella out of the way. "Nothing to see there. I assume we got all the pictures?"

"Should be in your file," Briggs replied.

Stella peered into the back of the van, taking in the locks and benches. Her eyes settled on a sliver of wood protruding from the far end of the seat cushion. What was that? She put a foot on the rear bumper to step up into the van and find out.

"Hey, I told you there's nothing up there. Let's get down to the morgue." MacGregor gestured toward the sedan. "Actually, why don't you go wait in the car?"

Stella met his gaze and stood her ground. "Doesn't hurt to have another pair of eyes inside."

MacGregor glared at her.

The crackle of the radio in Briggs's car broke the tension. A dispatcher's voice said something Stella didn't catch. Detective Briggs leaned into the window and picked up the microphone. "Yeah, this is Briggs. What have you got?"

Stella took her foot off the bumper and walked over to his side to listen.

"Thought you should know. A fingerprint match came in from one of the corpses you wanted identified. Came back as a guard at Polk Penitentiary named George Wallace," the dispatcher said.

"Well, that's good news. Do they want to send someone down to ID him?"

"There's been some confusion about that. They're pretty sure it's not him."

"Until they get down here, they won't know for sure."

"They said they're sure," the dispatcher replied. "They said George Wallace showed up for work today."

2 / THE MORGUE

"I THOUGHT I TOLD YOU TO KEEP YOUR MOUTH SHUT OUT there," MacGregor said as he closed the car door.

"I'm here to do my job," Stella replied. "To investigate."

MacGregor faked a smile as he waved out the car windshield to Detective Briggs, then pulled into the road to follow him. His features hardened when he looked back to her. "Don't get any grand ideas in your head about what you're doing here. Your job is to make the Bureau look good with the press and this Affirmative Action bullshit. I know Director Webster and his crew are all gung-ho about getting blacks and women in the door, but don't think that's the same thing as having real experience. You need to let the men do their jobs."

"You're really inspiring, MacGregor. You ever stop to think that maybe not everyone wants a good ol' boy agency anymore? You ever think that women and minorities might actually have something to offer?"

"Last thing I need is some rookie straight out of the academy giving me lectures, York. While you're assigned to me, I'm in charge," MacGregor said. "You follow my lead or I write you up for insubordination, you got it? You make the coffee, you get the reports in, and we'll get along well enough till I can dump you off on the next chump. That's your job. Until that happens, I don't want you getting in the way."

Stella crossed her arms and stared at the taillights ahead of them.

"I didn't hear a response, York. I want you to answer when I give you instructions."

Stella turned and glared at him. "I got the message."

"Sir," MacGregor replied. "I got the message, sir."

He wasn't wearing a seatbelt. Stella had the sudden urge to grab the wheel and push him out into traffic, but she contained herself. "I got the message, sir."

"Good," MacGregor replied. "Glad we got that straight."

MacGregor insisted on a pitstop at a fast-food burger place prior to proceeding.

While he walked inside, Stella pulled down the passenger side mirror and considered her reflection. Frowning, she fished around in her purse for a tube of lipstick. When she located it, she debated her options. This was another knife edge she had to walk in this job. Wear zero makeup and no man would bother to listen to what she had to say. Wear too much and no one took her seriously. Stella knew she caught more than a few eyes walking the halls of the Jacksonville office, but tended to tone down her looks for work.

In MacGregor's eyes, she was always going to be a *female* agent, not just an agent. It was obvious that in his mind she was taking a spot from a deserving man, but heaven forbid she wasn't still pleasant to look at.

Damn double standards.

She gave her lips a quick touch up and shoved the tube back in her bag before her partner lumbered back out the door.

He stared at her briefly when he climbed back into the car

but made no comment on her appearance, which was a relief. Once again, none the wiser.

When they reached the police station, Detective Briggs was waiting for them on the front steps. He had another file in his hands.

"They sort it out?" MacGregor asked, wiping French fry grease on his pants. "Somebody mess up the fingerprints?"

The detective shook his head. "Triple-checked. It's a definite match. All ten fingers. Never seen anything like it."

"Clerical error," MacGregor replied. "Somebody switched the guy's records."

Detective Briggs led them to the door and opened it for them. "Let's hope. We're going to find out in a minute. I had the penitentiary fax over everything they had on Wallace. Even got an updated photo. They developed it today." He handed the file to MacGregor. MacGregor skimmed through a few pages, then handed the file off to Stella. "Hold that."

When they reached the door to the morgue, MacGregor turned to Stella. "You want to wait outside for this? Might be rough on your constitution."

"I'll be fine," Stella replied, and resisted rolling her eyes.

MacGregor shrugged and followed Detective Briggs inside.

The bodies were already on display for them, a coroner's assistant on hand to help. The young man smiled and waved as they approached. "Figured you might be back to see these two."

"Tommy, these are Special Agents MacGregor and York from the FBI, here to take over the investigation."

"Then you have your work cut out for you," Tommy replied. "Double homicide by a mystery prison escapee. Don't get too many of those around here." He stepped over to the table and pulled back the sheet covering the first body, revealing the head and torso of a man who was likely in his fifties. His hair was graying and he had a bald spot at the crown of his head. He wore a mustache in the fashion of Tom Selleck, though the resemblance stopped there. This man was significantly shorter with a belly that protruded several inches beyond his chest.

Stella flipped open the file and removed the new photo of George Wallace that the prison had faxed over. They weren't a match. While their features were the same, the man in the photo had to be at least twenty years younger.

MacGregor snatched the photo from her and looked it over. "He's a relative. Father and son, maybe. They both work for the prison and they mixed up the fingerprint records." He turned to Stella and gestured to her. "Give me the prints." Stella located the sheet of images that had been faxed over, as well as the ones that had been taken from the corpse. Another sheet showed full and partial prints pulled from the crash site. MacGregor scanned back and forth between them, searching for an irregularity. "Has to be a mistake," he muttered.

"Polk County says George Wallace lives alone," Stella read from the file. "Divorced. No children. Father died in '68."

"Sure looks like him," Detective Briggs replied. "After twenty years of not taking care of himself, maybe. But it looks like him."

"What about the other one?" Agent MacGregor said, striding over to the second corpse.

The coroner's assistant pulled back the sheet. "This one's still a John Doe. No record we can find anywhere."

Stella followed her partner to the second table and studied the face of the other victim. He was young, early thirties, perhaps. His boyish jawline reminded her a lot of her older brother. They'd be about the same age too. The bruises on his neck showed evidence of the strangulation. The marks were an eerie yellow and purple in the morgue lights.

"I want to nail this guy," she muttered.

"What's that?" MacGregor replied.

"Whoever did this," she said. "He's got to go."

MacGregor shoved the paperwork into her hands and addressed Detective Briggs. "We got a number for this Wallace guy? The one who showed up for work at the prison?"

"It's in the file," Detective Briggs replied.

"Okay. Let's get him down here. We'll see what he says about his doppelgänger. He has to know something." He stared at Stella. "Get him here tomorrow. The sooner the better." MacGregor turned and stalked toward the doors.

Stella took another look at the young John Doe on the table. When she looked up she found Detective Briggs studying her. His expression was sympathetic. He looked like he was about to say something when MacGregor shouted from the doorway. "Let's go, York! Haven't got all night."

Stella nodded to the detective, then followed MacGregor back to the car.

3 / FIRE STARTER

The motel on Fourth Street wasn't much to look at. The TV was busted in Stella's room and the comforter on the bed looked like it was used to mop up a crime scene, but it had one glorious attribute. She didn't have to share it with MacGregor.

It was rare to be working in another Florida division, but the local Tampa field office was swamped and had asked for extra manpower. Normally she wouldn't have minded the change of scenery from the Jacksonville office, but she wished she could have ended up in charge of choosing the accommodations.

After the morgue, MacGregor had insisted on fast-food again, then coming straight back to the motel. The upside was that he'd asked Stella to drive, so he could start eating in the car. As a result, she still had the keys to the Ford.

She'd already reviewed the files from Detective Briggs and she had a head start on notes for her reports, but the van details still bothered her. She mulled over the case for a while, then tried going to sleep, but her mind wouldn't let her. After forty minutes of tossing and turning, she gave up. With the TV broken and nothing else to think about, she knew she wasn't going to be able to distract herself. She dressed in jeans and a comfortable sweater, then pulled her jacket on as she headed for the car.

When she got to the site of the van crash, she found the scene vacant. She pointed the headlights at the strangely undamaged power pole and climbed out to have a closer look. She walked all the way around it, scanning all sides, then pressed a fingernail into the wood and stripped away a sliver. There seemed to be nothing unusual about the pole. Certainly no reason it should have miraculously survived being struck by a van.

A uniformed officer was parked near the end of the block. After Stella climbed back into the car, she pulled up next to him and flashed her badge. "Hey, you know where they took the van from the crash?" She jotted down the address when he gave it to her and rolled on.

The impound was a sprawling, fenced-in lot that took up an entire city block. Cruising by a locked gate, Stella caught sight of the van sitting alone at the end farthest from the entrance. She parked the Crown Victoria on a side road and walked to the security gate. She had to ring a bell. The security guard showed up a few minutes later and stared at her credentials for a while, then at her. "Never seen a girl FBI agent before," he said. "Don't the feds usually wear suits and ties?"

"Not tonight," Stella replied.

It took him roughly an eon to get the gate open, but finally it yawned wide.

"Wonders never cease," she muttered.

She did a careful walkaround of the van when she reached it, jotting notes. When she opened the back, she needed her flashlight to see anything. Climbing inside, she swept the beam over the cushion to the sliver of wood she had spotted before. The tiny tear in the fabric looked like it had been there a while and she could see how the team removing the body wouldn't have paid it much attention. She donned a glove and removed the splinter of wood from the cushion. Only it wasn't a splinter. It was a matchstick. It was unburned but looked like it might have been chewed on. There were indentations on one end that could be teeth marks. She retrieved an evidence bag from her jacket pocket and tucked it inside.

She swept her light over the rest of the van, noting the dent in the side of the panelling where the victim must have impacted the wall. There was nothing else that caught her eye. She climbed back out of the van and closed the doors, then made her way slowly back to the guard shed.

"So, FBI, huh?" the security guard said. "How do I get into that?"

Stella did her best to keep her responses short, but the guard must have been bored, or perhaps lonely. He managed to keep up the conversation for more than ten minutes, pestering her about the job and what kind of cases she worked. Finally she insisted he open the gate and let her through. "I've got to get going. It's late."

"Okay, you come back anytime you like, all right? Maybe I'll see you at the Bureau one day."

"Good luck with that," Stella replied. "Be safe now."

She fastened her jacket tighter and headed down the sidewalk, making her way slowly back to the sedan. She wasn't in a hurry to return to the motel, since it would make it that much sooner that she'd have to deal with MacGregor. She got seated behind the wheel of the Ford and pulled the evidence bag from her pocket.

Perhaps she could compare the teeth marks in the matchstick to the victim's dental records? If it didn't belong to the guard, it could very well be her perp. She'd have to chat with Briggs in the morning.

Stella laid the bag on the passenger seat and leaned forward to twist the ignition key, but as she did so, she caught sight of movement down the street at the edge of the impound lot. Two men were exiting a gap in the fence. One was short and possibly Middle Eastern, the other was a tall Caucasian man with an athletic build and unruly brown hair. He was wearing a Gremlins T-shirt. Both men climbed aboard a sun-faded pink scooter. The shorter man donned a helmet and fired up the scooter.

"What the hell were you two up to?" Stella muttered. She started the car, pulling out to follow the two men. She kept her distance as she tailed them, not sure she wanted to reveal her presence yet. The scooter wasn't hard to keep up with. It was low powered and the duo couldn't be going far in this cold. The man on the back looked like he was shivering as it was. She tried to note the plate number on the scooter but the tag light was out and the shadow of the man on the back obscured it from the passing streetlights.

As she neared a stoplight, sirens blared and lights flashed in her rearview mirror. A fire truck blasted by, making its way toward a glow down the street. When Stella crested the hill and reached the intersection, the men on the scooter turned west. The street ahead was a riot of color as the light from a dozen emergency vehicles illuminated the night. Firemen were battling an inferno consuming a single-story office building. She spotted several police officers on the sidewalk across from the burning building. Detective Briggs was among them.

Stella weighed her options. The scooter with the two trespassers was buzzing away down the street. They could be a lead, or they could have been punks out to steal hubcaps. The roaring inferno could also be unrelated to her case too, but Detective Briggs was there for a reason. She couldn't help but wonder what that was. She glanced at the matchstick in the evidence bag next to her, then pulled the car over, grabbed the bag, and got out.

"We've gotta stop meeting like this, Agent York," Detective Briggs said as she walked up. "No partner tonight?"

Stella pulled her eyes from the blazing building. "He had other plans. You part of the fire brigade now?"

The detective stepped away from the other officers to join

her. "It's looking like another homicide, actually." He glanced down the sidewalk and Stella noted a crew loading a stretcher into the back of an ambulance. Detective Briggs walked her toward a vehicle parked on the opposite side of the street that had a law office sign rammed through the window. It was still smoking. "Some kind of explosion. One confirmed casualty so far. Victim's name was Alan Waters."

Stella studied the burning sign. "Lawyer, huh? Somebody have a beef with one of his cases?"

"Could be," Briggs replied. "But we usually see more violence against prosecutors. Waters mostly worked defense. Stand-up guy. Knew him from the courthouse. Everyone thought he had a bright future. Probably a judgeship, maybe politics eventually. Not anymore."

"Sorry to hear that," Stella replied. "Were you close?"

"Just close enough to shoot the shit. But he was one of us." Detective Briggs stuffed his hands in the pockets of his jacket and rolled his shoulders as if to shrug off the darkness.

Stella reached into her pocket and removed the evidence bag. "Found this in our mystery van. Any chance your forensics could get me an analysis of the teeth marks in it? Or maybe saliva? Curious to see if it's from one of the victims."

Detective Briggs took the bag and studied the marks. "Yeah, I've got a guy who could run some checks. This might be too small of a surface to pull from but I can ask. Could be from our escapee, huh?"

"We can hope," Stella replied.

"Looks like maybe you work better as a solo act. Ol' MacGregor slowing you down?"

"MacGregor hasn't quite embraced the idea of women in law enforcement yet. Any decade now he'll get the picture."

"Where'd the Bureau put you guys up?" Detective Briggs asked.

"Little motel on Fourth and Sixth. I'm blanking on the name. Has a tree involved."

"I know the place," Briggs replied. "I think I've arrested a few cockroaches there."

"The Ritz it ain't," Stella replied. "But MacGregor got to pick it and he's as cheap as they come."

"What's your room number?" Briggs asked. "I'll give you a call if I get anything back on the matchstick." He pulled a pen and notepad from his pocket.

Stella gave him the room number, trying not to read anything into his request. She presumed his interest was only professional, but she realized she would certainly pick up the phone either way. She looked him over as he scribbled. She hadn't had time for many extracurricular activities lately, but he was definitely her type. That great hair. Broad shoulders. Sincere eyes. It was clear he stayed in shape.

Briggs put away the pen and smiled at her. She realized he had asked her a question.

"I'm sorry, what?"

"You want me at the meeting with Wallace tomorrow?"

Wallace. Her dead van driver.

"Yep. Thanks. That would be great."

A fireman dragged a hose over and got ready to blast the vehicle next to them and put out the smoldering sign. Stella and Detective Briggs ended up on opposite sides of the hose. "Excuse me, folks," the firefighter said amiably. "Coming through."

Detective Briggs backed away toward his fellow officers, but before he did, he gave Stella a quick two-fingered salute. "See you tomorrow, Agent York."

Stella waved back. "Right. Goodnight, Detective."

"Call me Danny," he replied.

She smiled. "Goodnight, Danny."

He grinned.

She took one last look at the wreck of a building, then turned back toward the car. The sound of the fire hose inundating the car trailed her as she walked.

When she pulled the company sedan back onto the road, she took one last pass by the impound lot. She cruised by the spot she'd seen the two men exit the fence. They could have been anybody. Probably nothing to do with her mystery van. But as she drove back to the motel, she couldn't shake the feeling that she'd made the wrong decision in not following them. She could only hope that whoever they were, they'd show up again. When they did, she'd be ready.

4 / WALLACE

"Get that thing away from me!" George Wallace exclaimed. "It's unnatural!"

The prison guard had been driven to the station early but looked like he would be fleeing toward the door before long.

"Mr. Wallace, please calm down if you can," Stella said. "We just need to ask you a few questions."

"That's not me," Wallace said. "It's not me." He shook his head violently. "Somebody's idea of a sick joke. That's what that is. Let me out of here."

Agent MacGregor glared at the man as if willing him to spurt answers. "You mean to tell me you never seen this guy before? Ever?" He walked over to the second body and pulled back the sheet. "And this one?"

Wallace looked like he might be sick.

"So help me, if you throw up in here, I'll flatten you," MacGregor muttered.

Detective Briggs was in the hallway when Stella left the room.

"Good morning, Danny."

"That doesn't sound like it's going well in there." He was leaning casually against the doorframe of the morgue break room.

"I'm going to get him some coffee and see if I can settle him down."

Danny looked at the cup in his hand. "Coffee's pretty terrible. But if you're looking to play bad cop . . ."

Stella walked to the coffee pot and began pouring a cup. She muttered a curse when a few drops splashed out and ended up on her slacks. She was back in work clothes this morning, a white blouse and low, sensible heels. The look was all business, but she had made a little extra effort with her curling iron in anticipation of running into Danny.

"Any big New Year's Eve plans for tonight? You and MacGregor gonna paint the town red?" he asked.

Stella laughed. "That would be a grand end to 1985. Probably about fitting though, the way things have been going." She took a whiff of the coffee, then cringed. "Ugh. You weren't kidding."

Danny leaned closer. "Well, me and a couple of the narcotics guys are probably going out to—"

"Hey, Briggs!" The call came from the hall and another detective appeared in the doorway. "Chief's looking for you. You're working the Waters homicide, right?" He handed a file to Danny.

"Not right this second I'm not." Danny frowned.

"Well, you'd better get back on it. We've got another body, and they think it could be your guy's work."

"Another explosion?"

"No, but they found ammonium nitrate residue in some footprints. Same as the Waters fire."

Danny turned to Stella. "Sorry, looks like I gotta run."

Stella waved him off. "Good luck. I'll just be here poisoning my only lead." She lifted the cup of coffee.

Danny smiled, then followed the second detective down the hall.

Stella watched them disappear down the stairwell. "Happy New Year," she muttered.

"I'm getting tired of this nonsense!" Agent MacGregor shouted as he paced back and forth across his motel room. The dingy shag carpet was in danger of being worn away by his fury.

"We could try looking into wider possibilities," Stella said. "Some kind of human cloning?"

"Don't give me more bullshit to deal with," MacGregor said. "There is always an answer, and nine times out of ten it's some cock up we've failed to account for."

"Just trying to think outside the box. You know the Sherlock Holmes quote 'When you have eliminated the impossible—'"

"The *impossible* is not our job," MacGregor growled. "Get your head back to reality. That's what I get for having a woman for a partner. A mind in fantasy land."

Stella narrowed her eyes, but then let her gaze fall to the prints in front of her and shuffled them around. "Well, call it what you want. We've confirmed it's not a mistake with the analysis. The prints we got off Wallace today are a dead match with the body. There's no way that should be possible, even if it was some long lost identical twin. *You* explain it."

MacGregor ran his hands through his graying hair. "I still think this local PD is jacking the evidence up. We'll have to explain that in the reports." He turned to Stella. "I want you to get everything you can on these dead guards. And I want to keep eyes on this Wallace character. I don't care what he says, he has to know something."

"That reaction seemed sincere to me," Stella replied.

MacGregor glared at her. "We're going up to Polk County to nose around. We'll see if any other guards up there know something. Pack your shit."

"You want to go tonight? It's New Year's Eve."

"I doubt this scumbag we're chasing is taking the night off," MacGregor replied. "He could be anywhere by now. The sooner we have real evidence, the sooner we can get this case behind us. The prison is our only lead right now."

Stella closed the file. "Five bucks says we're back here by the weekend."

MacGregor grunted. "The prison will give us something. Mark my words."

It was the middle of the next week when MacGregor finally admitted defeat. Stella wanted to believe it wasn't just the five dollar bet that had inspired him to stay so long in Polk county, but there was little other explanation.

The other guards were no help. There was very little to be said about Wallace that they didn't already know. A week's worth of investigating and interviews had revealed that any skeletons he had in his closet were as uninspiring as the man himself. They'd brought Wallace more notoriety with their presence than he'd enjoyed in his entire career. Despite all of MacGregor's determination, they had come up empty. Thursday night found them back in St. Petersburg. Stella was grateful that at least they'd landed a different hotel.

When MacGregor was firmly ensconced in his room with the TV Guide, Stella picked up her room phone. She dialed the number and was pleased to hear Danny pick up.

"You have good timing. I was just locking up my desk."

"Afraid someone will solve all your cases before you can?"

"You're right, I should leave it open. How'd your trip inland go? Any leads?"

"All dried up."

"Sounds like you could use a drink," Danny said. "Come out with me tonight. I know a place with a good crowd. You can show me how well federal agents hold their liquor."

Stella wrapped the phone cord around her hand a few times. "Don't you know they issue iron gullets with our badges these days?"

She could hear Danny's smile as he spoke. "Forty-ninth Street Mining Company. You want to meet me there or can I give you a ride?"

"I do prefer to be chauffeured. I'll be outside the lobby in . . . twenty minutes."

"See you then."

5 / 49TH STREET MINING COMPANY

Danny wasn't lying about the crowd. Stella slung her purse over her shoulder as she got out of the car. It didn't match her outfit and wasn't her first choice for accessories, but she had to put her gun somewhere. She hadn't packed any dresses for this trip, but she had managed to include a herringbone-patterned pencil skirt and a blouse that fit her well. The sleeves were a little puffy for her taste and lacked the shoulder pads many other women were sporting tonight. She likewise wasn't in competition with the number of perms in attendance. The amount of Aqua Net that had been employed by men and women here was likely making the scene a fire hazard. She'd barely had time to give her hair a few extra curls before she was due outside the motel. Danny wasn't spending much time looking at her hair anyway.

"You brought me to a karaoke bar?" she asked as he led the way inside.

"This is the place to be tonight," Danny replied. "Drinks are cheap, the music is loud, and the scenery is a dream if you don't mind me saying so." He winked at her.

Stella wasn't quite sure what to make of this after-hours Danny Briggs just yet, so she let the comment pass without response. He had his jacket sleeves pushed up to his elbows and hadn't bothered with the top three buttons of his shirt. "You going to sing for me tonight?"

"I was hoping you'd sing for me."

"Now you're really dreaming," Stella laughed.

A pair of guys with bleached hair down to their waists were exiting a high-top table, so Danny guided them to it.

"See if you can hold this down for us," Danny said. "I'll go get us some drinks."

"All right."

"They're like piranhas in here. Don't let them steal my seat."

"Don't worry. I'll pistol whip anyone who tries," Stella said. She slid onto the stool as Danny began to elbow his way through the crowd to the bar.

The DJ picked up the microphone. "And next up, we've got Carson and . . . looks like Ben . . . singing, *You've Lost that Loving Feeling* by the Righteous Brothers. Come on up, Carson and Ben."

Stella watched as two young men edged their way to the stage, cheered on by several women at a table near the back. A dark-haired Latina woman whooped loudly.

It wasn't until the two men reached the stage and turned around that Stella recognized him. The tall, brown-haired man was even wearing the same Gremlins T-shirt she'd seen him in before. It was her quarry from the week before that had buzzed away on the back of a scooter.

The two young men began belting out a version of the Righteous Brothers song she hadn't heard done before and the crowd was eating it up.

Danny made it back with drinks around mid-song and Stella had to pull her attention from the stage to accept the glass from him.

"You know those guys?" Danny asked as he set his beer on the table.

"I think I want to talk to them," Stella said. "The tall one."

"I guess maybe I will have to sing tonight," Danny said. "Have I got competition already?"

Stella rolled her eyes. "I spotted him at the impound lot the night I saw you downtown. The night of the fire. There's a chance he might know something."

"You think he's a suspect?"

"I don't know yet."

When the two men finished their song, they hopped off the stage amid a raucous round of applause from the crowd.

Stella slipped off her stool and began to work her way toward them.

"You want backup?" Danny said.

"No. Your turn to fight off the table piranhas. I'll be right back." She hoisted her purse strap higher on her shoulder, her underarm pressing it tightly against her side.

The bar was a cloud of smoke and neon lights, so seeing her way to the back was harder than she anticipated. She aimed for the rear table where she'd seen the cheering women. When she got there, she was disappointed to find that the men at the table looked different. The red-haired one looked the same, but the tall, dark haired one was a completely different guy. No Gremlins shirt. The red-headed man was now chatting across the table with several blondes with teased out hair and matching jean jackets who seemed enamored by the performance. Where had the other singer gone?

The red-head caught Stella looking at him and smiled. "Hi. How's it going?"

Stella tried to seem spontaneous. "Hey. Great song!" She had to shout over the noise of the next performer beginning their rendition of Queen's *Another One Bites the Dust*.

"We figured it was a crowd pleaser." The man extended his hand. "I'm Carson. What's your name?"

"Stella. You guys locals?" She noted the Latina woman sizing her up and smiled back at her. The woman looked away.

"We've actually come quite a way to be here," Carson replied. "Bit complicated. You need a drink?"

"Um, sure. I'll have whatever you're having."

Carson guided her to the bar and ordered them two domestics. "You know, in a few years there's going to be a great local beer scene here," Carson said. "A couple of the guys I went to high school with have been making some great IPAs in their garage. They want to open a brewery themed around the old green benches they used to have down on Central Ave."

"You're into brewing?" Stella asked.

"Not really. But I like the drinking part." Carson clinked his bottle against hers. "Cheers."

"Looks like you have a good group of friends out tonight. You in town visiting?"

"We're mostly all from here, actually," Carson replied.

"But you said you've come quite a ways to be here? Which one is it?" Stella asked. She kept an eye out for the man she had seen on the scooter but he was still nowhere in sight. Per the DJ, if this one was Carson, then the other one must be named Ben. Danny was staring at her from their table on the other side of the bar looking sullen. She'd have to make this quick.

The DJ called into his microphone. "And next up we have Tanya and Tasha!"

Carson had to lean in close to make himself heard. "I'm from here but not *here*, here. I'm what you might call an anomaly. If I told you the whole story, you'd never believe me."

"Man of mystery, huh? Why don't you try me? I love mysteries."

But before he could answer, the two blonde women rushed up to him and began begging him to come sing with them. Carson attempted to deter them but Tanya and Tasha were determined to get him back on stage. Carson mouthed an apology as the girls put a microphone in his hand and dragged him in front of the crowd. The next minute all three were belting out the words to *Billie Jean* by Michael Jackson. Carson even threw in a moonwalk.

Stella made her way back to Danny. His drink was empty.

"Get ditched?" he asked.

"Guess I can't compete with the Doublemint Twins," she replied. "But he wasn't the one I was hoping to talk to anyway." She glanced around the bar, looking for the man from the scooter, but when she spotted him, she noted that he was deep in conversation with his Latina friend.

Danny lifted his glass and rattled the ice cubes. "Are we ready to stop working and start drinking? Or do you have more barflies to interrogate?"

Stella smiled and slid back onto the stool. "Ready when you are."

It was nearing midnight when Stella stepped outside into the cool night air. It was the middle of winter but she was barely chilled. Florida latitude and Kentucky Bourbon had conspired to keep her warm. Danny's hand pressed to the small of her back helped too.

"I was thinking that maybe you don't have to go back to that ratty motel tonight," Danny said, letting his hand linger on her hip. "I feel like maybe you owe it to yourself to get some better accommodations."

"I bet you know a place?" Stella said. "Maybe at a place you happen to live?"

"I mean it's not fancy," he said. "But we could have another drink and get comfortable there. See how you like it?"

"I think it's a great idea," Stella replied. She slipped her hand into his as they made their way toward Danny's car.

It would have been a beautiful and promising night if it weren't for the red and blue lights flashing in the parking lot. The broad-chested officer was standing outside a squad car, talking on the radio. He looked up and spotted Danny, then waved. Stella frowned.

The officer came over to greet them. "Hey, Danny. You may want to get over to 16th Street. Fire department is responding to a call over there. Suspected arson at a gas station. Proprietor is real shaken up from someone throwing gas on him and trying to torch the place."

"Anybody hurt?" Danny asked.

"No. Not that I heard. But if you want I can give you a ride down there."

"They need more eyes on it?"

"Yeah, you should probably come down. They think there's some danger of an explosion and they could use a few more hands to search for the guy."

Yep. There went her night.

The officer turned to study Stella.

"Oh. John, this is Special Agent York with the FBI. She's on the escapee case. We were just doing some . . . collaborating. "

"Nice to meet you, ma'am," the officer replied. "If you want, I can give you both a lift, assuming you don't mind the back."

Stella glanced toward the bar, then to Danny. "You know what? You go on. My head is a little fuzzy for field work tonight. I can get a cab back to the motel."

"You sure?" Danny asked. He stepped closer and lowered his voice. "If you wanted to go back to my place, I could meet you. I feel bad leaving you here so late."

"Don't worry. I can take care of myself," Stella replied. "You can fill me in tomorrow."

Danny seemed to be having trouble making up his mind, but finally agreed. "All right. I'll give you a call in the morning. We'll uh..."

"Collaborate?" Stella suggested.

"Right." Danny gave her hand a quick squeeze before scooting around the squad car to climb into the passenger seat. Stella waved once as the car pulled away.

So much for romance.

A payphone on the side of the building was free but she wasn't ready for a cab yet. She headed back toward the bar. Just as she was reaching the door, three of the friends she'd been keeping an eye on came spilling out. The one named Ben and his other tall friend were propping up a shorter man with a shaved head. "I'm telling you that if I could come up with an idea like that, I could retire right now. Leg warmers? I mean who thought of that?" The young man caught Stella's eye only briefly before carrying on. "After we save my grandpa, I'm gonna—" He cut himself off when Ben elbowed him.

The drunken friend looked up at her and smiled.

"Sorry. Were you headed in?" The second tall man released his grip on his friend and backed up a step to open the door for her. As he did so, their Latina friend emerged from the doorway with a scowl on her face.

"Let's get out of here already," she said as she rifled through her handbag and extracted car keys.

"Where's Carson?" the man holding the door asked.

"The hell if I care," the girl replied. "Maybe you can pry him away from Goldilocks and her extra clueless sister." She looked up to find Stella standing there and it didn't improve her disposition. "Oh. You again."

The man holding the door peeked back inside. "Yeah, maybe I should go retrieve him..."

Stella turned toward the man from the scooter. "Hi. Ben was it? I caught your Righteous Brothers rendition in there. Nice job."

The man smiled. "Oh, thanks. That was mostly Carson. He has an obsession with *Top Gun*."

"Top what?" Stella asked.

"Gun," the shorter, drunk friend explained. He had regained the ability to stand on his own. "The movie. You should know that one here. It's an 80s classic."

"Must have missed it."

"Shit," Ben muttered, elbowing his friend. "Probably not out yet."

"What's that?" Stella asked.

"Ohhh," the shorter friend took on a grave expression and pantomimed zipping his lips.

"I'm going to the car. You guys coming or what?" the girl said, jingling the keys.

"Yeah, we're right behind you," Ben said. He turned to Stella and smiled. "Nice to meet you. Have a great night."

Stella watched them make their way toward an old boat of a car in the parking lot. A Buick? She made a mental note of the license plate number. She was still rummaging around in her purse for her notepad and a pen when the other tall one and Carson reemerged from the bar.

"I'm not saying I wrote it, but if I sing it first and produce it, I still think that would technically make it *my* song." Carson was still talking when he saw Stella. "Oh, hey. You're still here. You waiting for a ride?"

Stella shouldered her purse. "My ride turned into a pumpkin. But I'll be fine."

Carson eyed the pad of paper and pen in her hand. "I'm afraid we don't do autographs."

Stella laughed. "I saw your dance moves in there. Maybe you should."

Carson grinned. "Oh, hey, Blake, this is my new friend..."

"Stella." She extended a hand. Blake shook it politely.

A car horn blared from the parking lot.

"Uh, it's great meeting you," Blake said. "Sorry we have to run. Our friend seems like she's had enough fun for one night."

Stella nodded. "Another time, perhaps."

Carson raised a finger. "That might be more likely than you think."

Blake clapped him on the back. "Come on. Fresca's waiting. We gotta roll."

The duo crossed the parking lot and piled into the old Buick.

A belt squealed as the woman behind the wheel shifted into gear and eased the big car forward. The headlights swept across Stella, causing her to squint before the car swung left and out to the road. She watched it dip into the street, then turn south. She waited until the taillights had disappeared before lifting her notepad and scribbling the plate number.

She jotted the names down too. Ben... Carson... Blake... and Fresca?

Tonight may not have gone as planned, but for all the difficulty of the case so far, her gut was finally telling her she had a lead worth investigating. She didn't know what to make of it yet, but she would soon.

She walked into the phone booth, picked up the receiver, and dialed herself a cab.

6 / DISAPPEAR

"I'm sorry about the other night." Detective Danny Briggs was looking solemn. "I should have stuck around."

Stella was working at a borrowed table in the police headquarters conference room, reviewing the latest additions to the case file.

"It's the job. You don't have to beat yourself up about it."

"You get the info I sent on the gas station fire? We don't know if there is a connection to the van escapee yet but we're looking at everything."

"I've looked through most of it. I actually wanted to ask you something. I was reviewing the security camera footage but I feel like you're missing a big chunk of time." She picked up the VCR remote and aimed it at the rolling TV stand. "I get up to around one o'clock, then it cuts off. What's the story with that?" She reached the end of the tape, then hit the rewind button.

Briggs leaned against the wall and crossed his arms. "Yeah. Perp flipped the breaker on the building right after he chased the manager down the bathroom hallway. When someone turned the power back on, the CCTV required a manual restart to start recording again. We didn't get anything from the fire itself. Just the bit where the guy first walked through the door."

Stella flipped through the file on her desk. "Manager says he got rescued by a . . . 'barefoot guy in a jumpsuit who locked himself in the bathroom and then disappeared?' Who gathered that testimony?"

Danny sighed. "Officer Marks took that report but I was there too. Door was still locked when we got there. Manager swears a guy went in there and never came out. When we finally got the door open, the room was empty."

"So what's your take?" Stella asked. "Guardian angels?"

"I assume he slipped out when the manager wasn't looking," Briggs replied. "Must have locked the door behind him for some reason."

Stella flipped through the file in front of her. "Report says the back door was blocked by a dumpster. You didn't see anybody leave out the front?"

"Not that anyone noticed, but he had to have gotten out sometime. Maybe before we got there."

At that moment, Special Agent MacGregor barged into the room. "York, what do you think you're doing? I need you getting testimony from Polk County."

Danny raised his eyebrows, then eased himself out the door. Stella frowned, then turned to her partner. "The Wallace lead? We beat that into the ground already. He's a dead end."

"Toe tags on those stiffs in the morgue still say John Doe on 'em don't they? Is that what you call case closed?"

"I've run every lead on the bodies you gave me. No one has ever seen them before. You have something new?"

"I want *you* to come up with something new, not spend your time floozing it up with local PD. If you want to embarrass yourself, do it on your own time."

Stella opened her mouth to speak but MacGregor's expression was too eager. His jowls were practically quivering with anticipation. If she took the bait and unloaded on him, it would give him the perfect excuse to write her up. She'd worked too hard to let him get to her now.

"I'll finish this arson research and then get back on the Wallace angle."

MacGregor sniffed, seeming disappointed in her lack of confrontation. "I'm heading to the airport. Meeting with SAC Renfroe to report in and take a few days off. When I get back I hope you'll have made yourself useful."

"Yes, sir," Stella replied.

She waited till he was out of the room before she muttered the curses she was holding back.

She was happy he was leaving town, but had no confidence in him saying anything good about her work in his report to the Special Agent in Charge. She would have liked to be at the office in person to represent her own research but it was never going to happen.

She realized the video on the TV was still rewinding and caught an unusual flurry of activity beyond the fuzzy horizontal lines. She reached for the remote and hit the play button again. The time stamp on the camera feed showed just after seven pm. The proprietor of the station was leaning over a magazine, but looked up in alarm suddenly, then hurried to the back of the convenience store. A woman was guiding a little girl out of the bathroom. The child was clearly jabbering something but the video lacked an audio component. Whatever happened, she was flustered and kept pointing to the rear of the building. The mother had a worried expression on her face and gestured at the proprietor. The man quickly moved to the rear door of the store and out of frame. He came back perhaps ten seconds later and shook his head. The conversation continued for a few minutes before the woman hurried her daughter back out the front door.

Stella's curiosity was piqued. She rummaged around in the bag of tapes and found the one marked as the rear parking lot feed. She got up and popped it into the VCR. It took several minutes to find the corresponding time stamp, but sure enough, just as the appointed time came, the back door of the store opened and a barefoot man in a jumpsuit emerged.

"What the hell?" Stella leaned forward in disbelief as she watched the man exit the store, glance around the parking lot, then sprint out of frame. A few seconds later, the store proprietor stuck his head out the door to look around, then closed it again.

Stella rewound the video to the point the barefoot man was emerging and let it play again. She paused it when he was fully in view.

There was no doubt in her mind. It was the same guy from the scooter. The tall brown-haired young man she met at karaoke. Ben.

"What on earth are you up to?" she muttered.

She fast-forwarded through several minutes of footage, then rewound as well, looking for any other sightings, then switched back to the internal camera tape and searched as well. She found several other shots of patrons entering and exiting the bathroom hallway, but none with her suspect. Unless he was hiding in the bathroom for hours at a time, it seemed as though he appeared in the bathroom by magic, then ran out the back door a little after seven. Despite searching through the equivalent of several hours of footage, there was no sign of him ever entering the building. Frustrated, Stella rewound all the way to the beginning of the tape, and even checked the tape from the morning, but found no sign of him ever entering the store.

She looked through the police report for the proprietor's statement and reread it. She skimmed through the part about the patron attempting to douse him with gas and chasing him inside. The proprietor had then hid in the bathroom. He claimed the barefoot man rescued him from the bathroom just after the power went out, then went into the bathroom himself and locked the door, completely vanishing by the time the police got the door open.

Stella leaned back in her chair. He somehow came out of the bathroom after seven pm, but went in after midnight? It made absolutely no sense. She double-checked the time stamps and the proprietor's statement, but that's what it said.

Stella rewatched the video several times, studying the images of the arsonist as well, but found no new information. She checked the report again and noted the date.

She had been at the bar with Danny that night.

What time had she left the bar?

Briggs hadn't left till after he got the call about the fire. The karaoke singer had been there the whole time, hadn't he? It *couldn't* have been the same guy who let the proprietor out. It was completely impossible unless he was in two places at once. She jotted a note in her notebook. *Timeline makes no sense.*

She stared at the words. There seemed to be a lot of that going around this week.

It was 4:30 when a pretty young secretary in high-waisted slacks walked in with a print-out stuck to a clipboard. "Hi. Special Agent York? I have that license plate information you requested."

"Thank you," Stella replied, accepting the sheet of perforated printer paper the secretary offered. The woman lingered in front of the desk, staring. "Was there anything else?" Stella asked.

"No. Sorry. I just think it's rad what you do, you know? A woman in the FBI."

"It's not as glamorous as it might seem," Stella replied.

"But still," the secretary said. "You have a gun and a badge and work for a big federal agency. Around here if you're a woman trying to work in law enforcement, they just want to grab your ass or send you for coffee." She frowned. "I've been working here a year now. Sometimes I don't think it's ever going to get better."

"You been to college?"

"Two years."

"Major in political science and finish up your bachelor's degree, and then come apply at the bureau," Stella said.

"You really think they'd take me?" she asked.

"If they know what's good for them," Stella said.

"All right, then. Maybe I will." The young woman clutched her clipboard to her chest and smiled, then turned and walked out.

Stella watched the vacant doorway for a long second, hoping she hadn't set the young woman's expectations too high, but then shook off the thought. The MacGregor's of the world had to be on the way out. This was 1986. It was time for things to change.

She looked down at the printout in her hand.

The Buick was registered to a Robert Cameron. She copied the address into her notebook for ease of access and read on further. There wasn't much on him. No criminal record. Not even any traffic violations. She'd need to get a better look at the location and see how he was affiliated with the guy Ben from the bar.

She recalled the moment she spotted him exiting the impound lot. If they were running some kind of chop shop, it would be pretty stupid to be stealing from a police impound. Still, it was worth looking into. There was something very strange going on with this group of friends, and she was determined to find out what it was. She gathered up her notebook and moved to the door. She almost collided with Briggs on the way out.

"Oh, hey," Danny said. "Hoped you were still around. How'd the video research turn out? Any leads?"

"Implausible ones," Stella replied. "Hey, what time did you leave the bar the other night?"

"Uh, around midnight, I think, wasn't it?"

"That's what I thought. And the guys I was watching at the bar. You agree they were there the whole time, right?"

"You couldn't keep your eyes off them," the detective said. "Despite my best attempts to distract you."

"There's something not normal about that group."

Danny leaned against the wall. "You working tonight or do you want to maybe grab a drink? I promise not to get dragged away this time."

"Another night, maybe," Stella said. "I'm onto something here and I just need to figure out what it is."

"You think the guys from the bar have something to do with your prison escapee? How are you making that connection?"

"I saw one of them leave the impound lot where the prisoner van was held, then the same guy shows up connected to your arson case. I'm beginning to think it's all the same damn case," Stella replied.

"You think the arsonist is the same guy as our van killer?"

"I don't know for sure," Stella said. "But the things I don't know are starting to pile up. I plan to get some answers, and I'm going to start right now."

7 / PARADOX

Stella York took the freeway on-ramp at Fifth Avenue and headed north, grateful that MacGregor had at least left her the car and had the good sense to take a cab to the airport. She yielded to an elderly couple in a convertible who had the top down and seemed in no particular hurry as they merged onto Interstate 275. It would be a short drive to the next exit, then she could stop by the address in her notebook and see what she could learn about Robert Cameron and his Buick.

Stella attempted to change lanes to get out from behind the old folks in the convertible, but an eighteen wheeler and a passenger van were blocking her. She glanced ahead, trying to gauge whether it would be worth getting around them and the convertible or if there was even time before her exit. She changed to the middle lane and then nearly had a heart attack.

There was a man standing on top of the tractor trailer in front of her!

Stella gawked in amazement as she recognized the arsonist from the gas station surveillance video staggering along the top of the truck, working to keep his balance in the wind.

"What the hell?" Stella said, trying to get a better look at what was going on on top of the trailer. It was only a few car lengths ahead of her. She scrambled to grab her notepad and pen to write down the truck's tag number, but froze when she spotted the second man. He was crab walking backward near the edge of the trailer. She caught a glimpse of his face as he looked down at the old people in the convertible in the next lane. The old folks saw him too and began to point and shout. The arsonist from the station video was standing, wielding a knife, and he looked like he was about to fillet the guy laying atop the trailer.

"Holy shit!" Stella dropped her notepad and reached for the gun at her waist, but didn't even have time to clear it from her holster when the soon-to-be-victim on the top of the trailer promptly disappeared.

The man with the knife looked flabbergasted. Stella's jaw dropped too. She stared at the spot where the young man had just been but he had vanished. The man with the knife began to turn, raising the knife to look for his victim behind him, but he never got the chance.

The next moment was pure horror. A pedestrian overpass cleared the top of the truck but took the arsonist with the knife right in the back. He was launched headlong into traffic.

Stella swerved wildly across the fast lane and shoulder and bounced through the grass in the median between the northbound and southbound lanes, nearly losing her seat. By the time she regained control of the car she had spun sideways and was now angled toward the freeway facing the wrong direction. She jammed the brakes hard and skidded to a stop, the car rocking violently as it came to rest.

Other drivers weren't so lucky.

The freeway was chaos. Several cars had swerved out of their lanes and ended up in the runoff ditch, one embedded itself in the guardrail, and a few others collided with one another in the free-for-all on the road.

Stella slowly uncurled her fingers from the steering wheel,

secured her gun back in its holster, and swung the door open on her car. She took a second to calm her nerves and dizziness, and then climbed out to survey the carnage.

The big rig hadn't stopped.

She spotted the old couple in the convertible parked along the far side of the road a hundred yards farther along the freeway. The passenger van that had been behind Stella on the freeway had a shattered windshield and was halfway into the grass. The windshield was splattered with blood.

It was time to work.

Stella made sure traffic had completely stopped before rushing to assist the injured. The driver of the van was an airport shuttle driver who was severely shaken but seemed to be unharmed. Stella made her way from car to car and checked on the condition of the occupants. There were quite a few people with minor injuries and several cars that had suffered severe damage, but fortunately none of the occupants seemed to be in a critical condition.

Until she came to the body.

Several onlookers had gathered around the man, but no one had summoned the courage to touch him. Stella instructed the gawkers to step back and give her some room. "Someone needs to get to a phone, let emergency services know what happened right away!"

"I have a CB in the car," a man said.

"Use it," Stella replied. "Get on channel nine and call this in. Let them know we need ambulances on scene right away."

Stella crouched next to the fallen man's body and put her fingers to his throat to check his pulse. She knew the answer to the question without having to check, but she went through the motions anyway. The man's body was broken in places that you don't come back from.

Over the next few minutes, Stella did her best to reassure

drivers of the vehicles that had struck the man that the accident was unavoidable. By the time the first police cars and emergency responders showed up, she had made a mental list of the key witnesses. She was going to be one herself, but could she believe what she had seen? Where had the men come from and where did the other one disappear to? The image of the man on top of the truck came back to her and she recalled when he glanced down at traffic. Had it really been Ben? The same barefoot guy from the gas station fire? It had certainly looked like him. Whatever these two guys had going on, it seemed like they kept clashing in the most extreme ways.

Once emergency response was well under way and ambulances had begun gathering up the injured, Stella made her way over to one of the squad cars. "I need to get an alert out on another vehicle involved in the accident," she said. She pulled out her badge.

The officer looked interested. "FBI, huh? You have a lead on what caused all this?"

"Big rig trailer was headed north. This victim was on top of the thing when he got hit by the overpass. He's a suspect in an ongoing investigation we're involved with. I only have a partial on the plate for the big rig and a description of the trailer, but we should get a call in to see if someone spots it. I'd love to know where it came from."

The officer nodded and reached for the transmitter.

Stella spent the next thirty minutes giving her report to the officers on scene and reassuring the medical responders that she didn't need attention herself.

The body on the side of the road had been covered up but the area was still being photographed. The officer with the radio walked up to Stella and tapped her on the shoulder. "Hey. Thought you might like to know. Had a call in for a possible sighting of your truck. Someone saw it coming back across the

Gandy Bridge, then turning south on Ninth Street. They said it pulled back into a loading dock. Vicinity of Ninth Street and Fifteenth Avenue North."

"How long ago?"

"A couple minutes, maybe?"

Stella thanked the officer and made a note of the address, then checked her watch and made her way back to the rental car. In her report to the officers on scene, she had omitted the part about seeing a guy vanish into thin air atop the truck, but she still wanted to know what happened to him. Had she just lost sight of him? Was he still up there the whole time?

She climbed back into her car and eased it along the breakdown lane until she found a break in the guardrail, then swung the sedan into the southbound lanes and sped up to join the flow of traffic headed that way. It took her about ten minutes to reach the intersection the officer had listed.

Stella had the windows down as she cruised Ninth Street looking for the loading dock that the officer had mentioned, subsequently she smelled the smoke before she saw the fire.

What the hell was going on now?

Traffic was light but she came upon a couple of cars stopped along the side of the road. A young man was standing beside the vehicle of a passerby while pointing to a multi-story glass-paned office building across the street. He looked vaguely familiar but she couldn't place him. It looked as though he had flagged down the car and was looking for help. It was obvious why. Smoke was billowing out vents in the roof and the glow of flames illuminated several windows.

Stella climbed out of the car and walked briskly toward the man standing in the street. She flashed her badge as he turned toward her. He appeared to be Middle-Eastern with dark eyes and a distinctive crooked nose. She tried to recall where she had met him before. He looked relieved to see the badge. He immediately began gesturing toward the building.

"There's a crazy man in there. Very dangerous. He's holding people hostage and he lit the building on fire! Stenger. His name is Elton Stenger!"

"Has someone called the fire department?" Stella asked.

"The first car I stopped. They went to find a payphone," the man replied. Several bystanders had accumulated on the sidewalk now as well, gawking from the vicinity of the bus stop.

"You said there are hostages inside? How many?" Stella asked.

"Two. My friends Francesca and Ben. They're on the third floor."

Francesca and Ben. Them *again*? What on earth was going on with these people?

"Is there a loading dock for this building?" Stella asked.

"Around back," the man replied. "You might be able to get in that way. There's a back door. But you have to be fast."

"What's your name?" Stella asked the man.

"Malcolm. Malcolm Longines."

"Stay here, Malcolm. Tell the fire department and police what you told me as soon as they arrive. I'll be right back." Stella pulled her gun from its holster and darted across the street, angling toward the sidewalk that ran alongside the building.

In a situation like this, she had limited options. An arsonist with hostages inside a burning building? She needed backup. Backup she didn't have. She had no doubt that the police would be on scene any moment, but it might be too late. She needed to at least get a look at the situation, and then she could decide whether or not to go inside after the hostages.

Stella moved quickly down the sidewalk, trying several door handles along the side of the building, but they were all locked. When she was almost to the alley at the back of the building, she discovered the loading dock. The trailer she had seen earlier on the freeway was there, now missing its tractor. Whoever had been on top of it was—

Right there! The man she had seen disappear, Ben, was back again. Not in the building like the man Malcolm had said, but here on the ground. He was doing something strange, creeping along the alley, watching the windows on the third floor. Stella quickly ducked into the shrubbery along the path, hidden from his view, but able to observe. She kept her gun ready. What was he doing? The young man slunk along the alley until he reached a low wall with some bushes for cover and ducked behind it. She could still make out one of his feet protruding from his hiding place, but it was clear he was trying not to be seen.

A window overhead exploded. Glass shards rained onto the loading dock, along with two intertwined figures. They plummeted from the third story window and crashed onto the top of the trailer with a resounding thud.

Stella's heart leapt in her chest from the shock of the noise and she instinctively covered her head to protect from any more falling glass. The next moment she had her gun trained on the top of the trailer. One of the figures stood up.

It was impossible.

It was the same man from the alley. Ben. She turned toward where the young man had been hiding and could still see his foot protruding from behind the bushes. Now there were two of them? The man on top of the trailer had to be his twin.

The other man stood up as well.

Stella's stomach turned a flip in her gut.

It was the dead man from the Interstate. Her arsonist.

Stella lurched backward, colliding with the wall of the building. It was as though the ground was a rug that had suddenly been pulled out from under her. Her head spun and she slipped sideways and landed in the leaves and twigs behind the shrubbery. Her legs went to jelly and the gun fell from her fingertips. She struggled to stay alert. Oh God. What was happening to her?

Stella grasped at the shrubbery next to her, scratching herself in the face with dried limbs of the poorly watered plant as she tried to right herself and dispel her dizziness. She managed to keep herself upright long enough to regain a view of the top of the trailer. The two men were grappling atop the truck. The one called Ben tried to run, but the other man tripped him. Stella lost Ben to view, but heard the other man, Stenger, give a loud shout. The next moment everything went silent.

Stella's world flipped upside down. It was as though the sky was leaking out of the hole in the building above her. She was vaguely aware of sirens in the street. Unkempt shrubbery. A lizard watched her from its perch on the concrete wall of the building. Its throat extended in a colorful display of orange. Its gaze was pitiless.

Stella wanted to throw up. If she knew which direction the ground was in, she may have tried, but she felt like her mind was being siphoned backward through a straw. Her vision narrowed. Everything in the world was shrinking smaller and smaller until it was a single point of light. If there was anything else in the universe beyond that luminescent pin prick at the edge of her consciousness, it was failing to show itself. Stella realized it had been a very long time since she had taken a breath. Eons perhaps. She ought to try it. She gasped for air but there was none to be had. Then her universe went black.

8 / WAKE UP

STELLA BLINKED SEVERAL TIMES AND WAITED FOR HER EYES to focus. She wasn't dead. That was something. The room around her slowly took shape, synapses connecting in her brain to trigger the right memories, the right word for this place.

Hospital.

She was lying in a bed and two men were beside her. One was a doctor she didn't recognize. The other was a familiar face. Detective... Briggs.

"Good morning, Hot Shot," he said. "Welcome back to the land of the living."

Stella tried to sit up.

"Whoa, whoa," the doctor said. "No need to rush yourself. You've been through quite an ordeal. Just relax."

"Where—" Stella managed. She squinted in the morning sunlight streaming through the window.

"Where are you?" the doctor suggested. "This is St. Anthony's hospital, downtown. I'm Dr. Yearwood."

"No," Stella muttered. "Where did he go? The arsonist."

"Sorry, Doc," Danny said. "Always working, this one." He turned toward Stella. "Don't worry. Bureau says they have your case under control. Nothing to fret about."

"Can you tell me your name?" the doctor asked.

Stella blinked at him. "Um . . . Stella." The rest of her name. Must remember it. "Special Agent . . . Stella York," she corrected. "And I need to get out of here." She tried to sit up again and began looking for her clothes. Where had they put them?

"Special Agent York, you have suffered a very significant blackout," the doctor said, moving to block her exit from the bed. "I may need to run some tests on you before we let you go. I'd recommend lying back and resting for now."

Stella blinked at him, then slowly eased back against the pillows. Maybe a little rest wasn't a bad idea.

"Could you maybe give us a few minutes, Doc?" Danny said. "Just so I can fill her in on a few things? Won't take long. Then we can do those tests if she wants you to."

The doctor stood up straighter, checked his clipboard, then nodded to Detective Briggs. "All right, a few minutes isn't likely to hurt anything. Try not to agitate her at all. I'll be back in about five."

Danny waited till the doctor was out of the room before speaking. He sat on the edge of the bed and rested his hand on hers. "Gave us a bit of a scare there. When they found you they said you were in and out of consciousness. Do you remember what happened?"

Stella's memories were jumbled. Her head had a fuzziness to it that she couldn't place. It was like a hangover without the dehydration or headache. Everything was slow in coming to mind and seemed on the edge of slipping away.

"There was a building fire. After the accident."

The detective leaned closer. "We know about the building fire. What kind of accident?"

"The one on the freeway." The memories were coming back to her. "I saw him die, Danny. Our arsonist. But then he wasn't dead. Neither of them were."

"The gas station arsonist from the videotapes? You saw him get killed?"

"He was on top of the truck. On I-275. The pile-up. He was the one that caused it."

Detective Briggs pulled out his notebook and scribbled a few notes. "Pile-up, huh? What does it mean he died, but didn't die?"

"It was . . ." Stella tried to put it to words. "It was like things were happening out of order. I saw them end up on the truck. But it was *after* they were on it. Only I had already seen it. He was dead in the road. The other guy, Ben—the one we saw at the karaoke bar—he was on the truck too, but he disappeared."

"Afraid you're not making a lot of sense," Danny said. "Take your time. Do you remember how you ended up in the bushes? Some firemen found you unconscious in an alley. You have any idea how you got there?"

"Yeah. I was hiding," Stella replied. "Trying to see where the hostages were."

"Hostages? What hostages?" Danny asked.

"The ones the guy in the street was talking about. What was his name? Melvin? No. Malcolm. What happened to him?"

"Malcolm," Danny said, scribbling in his pad again. "I'll ask around if anyone saw him. Sounds like we have a lot more questions to ask."

It was nearing lunchtime when Stella was finally cleared to leave the hospital. The doctors wanted her to stay longer in case her incident had been something more serious, but Stella assured them that she felt fine and had merely fainted at the scene of the fire. She was lying of course. Whatever happened to her was shaking up her memories in a bad way, but she wasn't going to spend another day in the hospital if she could help it. She wanted answers.

She lingered on the sidewalk outside the hospital lobby and checked her watch. Detective Briggs had promised to pick her up, but hadn't arrived yet. An older man was seated in a wheelchair near her, apparently waiting for a ride as well.

"You escaped too, eh?" he asked cheerily. "Good for you. You have a ride?"

Stella smiled back. "I do. Thanks."

"Hope it was nothing serious," the man said. "Not that it's my business."

"It's all right," Stella replied. "I'll be fine. How about you?"

"Would've been dead if my grandson hadn't been around to help me," the man replied. "But luckily my story gets a happy ending today. Home in time for lunch." He looked up as a car pulled into the roundabout. "Ah. My getaway driver is here."

Stella turned to observe the car and it immediately arrested her attention. It was an old Buick. The same old Buick she had seen at the karaoke bar. It couldn't be the same one, could it? She couldn't recall the plate number.

But when the driver got out of the car, she immediately recognized him. He was the short young man with the buzzed hair who had been helped to the car by friends on account of being too drunk that night. She didn't recall his name but his features were easily recognizable. He was sober now and moved quickly around the car to help the old man out of his wheelchair.

"All right, Grandpa, let's get you out of here."

"You need any help?" Stella asked, moving closer.

"I think I got it," the young man said. He had a pleasant smile and eyes that resembled his grandfather's.

"This is my grandson, Robbie," the old man said. "He's a time traveler, you know."

"Grandpa!" the young man said. He turned to Stella with an apologetic smile. "Sorry. They have him on a lot of meds still."

"Oh, she doesn't care what I say," the old man said. "I'm just having a little fun. Gotta tell somebody."

Robbie got his grandfather seated in the Buick and then disappeared back inside the hospital with the wheelchair.

"He's been good to me," the old man said.

"We actually met the other night," Stella said. "Your grandson and I. Though I don't know if he remembers. It was a busy place."

"Oh, did you now?" the old man said. "Isn't that a strange coincidence?"

"I'm beginning to wonder," Stella replied. "Strange coincidences seem to be multiplying in my life this week."

The old man bobbed his head. "I've been alive a long time now," he said. "But there are things in the world that still surprise me. Things no one would ever believe if I told them. Do you know what that feels like?"

"Actually, I do," Stella replied. "More than you might imagine."

"Best keep our heads on straight then, eh?" He winked at her.

Stella closed the old man's car door as his grandson re-emerged from the hospital lobby and made his way around the vehicle.

Detective Briggs pulled into the roundabout a moment later, angling his Pontiac Trans Am into position behind the Buick.

"What's your name?" Stella asked the old man as she leaned down to address him through the window.

"Robert," He replied. "Robert Cameron. But my friends call me Lucky." He offered her a hand. "What do they call you?"

"Definitely not lucky," she replied, shaking his hand.

Robbie, the grandson, shifted the car into gear and gave her a polite smile.

Stella backed away from the car and gave the old man a wave. "Nice meeting you."

"You take care now," the old man said.

Detective Briggs shut the Pontiac's door and walked over to join her as the Buick pulled away from the curb. "You all set to go?"

"Yeah." Stella watched the big car pull back onto the street and into traffic. She turned to the detective. "You believe in coincidences?"

Danny pondered the question momentarily. "Sure. I mean it's a small world. Bound to happen, don't you think? Why? You know that old guy from somewhere?"

"Not yet," she replied. "But I have a feeling it's not the last I've seen of him."

Danny held the door for her as she climbed into his Trans Am.

"You aren't going to like the news I have for you," Danny said, as soon as he was behind the wheel.

"What news?"

"I put in a few calls around the station this morning. Nobody had any reports of this pile-up you mentioned. You sure it was bad enough that the department got calls?"

"Are you kidding?" Stella asked. "There was a body in the middle of the freeway. You couldn't get the report on that? Had to be at least a dozen officers on scene."

"Nobody I talked to seemed to know anything about it," Danny said. "You're sure it was in the city limits? Wasn't in Lealman or something, was it?"

"It was right in the middle of the Interstate, Danny. You obviously didn't ask around very well."

Danny headed toward the freeway. "Maybe you can show me the scene real quick, and talk me through what happened."

Danny was taking the same freeway on-ramp Stella had used

the night before. It was easy for her to narrate the events as they merged into northbound traffic.

"And there was a car ahead of me, a convertible with an old couple in it, so I tried to go left and then the tractor trailer..." she paused as the memory caused a twinge in her head. She winced.

"You okay?" Danny asked, looking over with concern.

"Yeah. I'm good." Stella shook off the strange sensation and focused on the road. "And right, up here, that pedestrian overpass. The truck went under it. That's what hit him." She scanned the median and guardrail. "There were cars all over the place. There ought to be an indent in the guardrail right where..." she paused as she realized she couldn't spot any damage. What the hell? She pivoted in her seat to try to look back and they went under the overpass. "Pull over, okay?"

Danny eased the car into the breakdown lane and rolled to a stop. Stella opened the car door and got out.

Where was it? What had happened to the dented guardrail? There's no way it had been fixed overnight.

Stella waited for a break in the traffic, then sprinted across the three lanes of freeway to the median.

"Stella! Wait!" Danny shouted.

But Stella was already back to the overpass and scanning the grass. Multiple cars had gone off the road. There ought to be tire tracks everywhere. Where in the hell were they?

Trucks barreled past on the freeway, rattling and roaring, while big blasts of air rushed by her. Stella pushed her hair away from her face and continued to search the median, jogging forward to the point where her car had slid to a stop the day before.

There was nothing. The grass hadn't been disturbed. There were no ruts or indents in the mud. What had happened to them?

Stella kept her hands to her head, pressing in the sides of her skull trying to force her eyes to see what they ought to see. She wasn't crazy. She knew what she saw. She doubled over as another twinge of pain shot through her skull.

"Hey, hey, take it easy over here," Danny said, grasping at her wrists and pulling her hands away from her head.

She looked up at him through strands of her hair and gasped the words. "It was right here, Danny. I saw what I saw!"

"Okay, okay," he said, wrapping her in his arms. "It's gonna be fine."

The feel of his arms around her should have been comforting but her mind was racing too fast.

The body. The aftermath of cars colliding with one another. It was too much. She never could have imagined such a scene in her dreams. It was too vivid. It was real.

"There's something wrong, Danny," she whispered, wrapping her arms around his back. "This isn't what happened."

STELLA WAS in a daze as they made their way downtown. Danny took her to his place and ushered her inside the one-story ranch house.

"I feel like you should get more rest," he offered. "I'll make you some coffee, or maybe tea. You can sort through all this stuff and make some sense of it."

"I ought to be down at the station talking to the officers who were on duty last night," Stella said. "I need to find the ones that were there at the scene."

"That's probably not a great idea right now," Danny said, glancing out the front window to the street. "I'll ask around if I go down there, but maybe it's best if you don't stir things up there just yet."

"You don't believe me," Stella said. "You think I'm making it up."

"That's not what I'm saying," Danny replied. "I don't know

what's going on with the car accident you mentioned. All I know is that I'm going to help you get to the bottom of it. I just think you should stay put for a bit before we go off half-cocked. Let's make a plan and see what we can figure out."

Stella admitted that wasn't the worst idea. Her head was still fuzzy and she needed to sit down. She eased herself into a recliner in the living room while Danny went in search of tea. Leaning to one side, she pulled her service pistol and holster from her belt and laid them on the coffee table next to her, then eased back into the cushions.

The moment she closed her eyes, the scene played out in living color in her mind. She was there. The traffic. The disappearing man, Ben. The man on top of the truck had been struck by the overpass right in front of her. He was absolutely dead. Someone had to be able to confirm it.

She opened her eyes. "We need to call the hospitals and the morgue," she shouted to Danny in the other room. "They'll be able to confirm an ambulance brought in a body. Elton Stenger. That's the name we're looking for."

"I'll make some calls," Danny said. The microwave dinged and he reemerged from the kitchen a minute later with a mug of hot water and a couple packets of instant tea. "Not sure which flavors you like."

Stella selected an Earl Grey and dropped the tea bag into the steaming cup. "I need to check in with my field office. You mind if I use your phone?"

"You ought to wait a bit. Clear your head," Danny suggested.

"You keep talking to me like I'm a crazy person," Stella snapped. "You don't have to baby me."

Danny raised his palms. "Hey, I'm just saying you might want to get your facts in order. Present it in the best light once you know a few more details.

"Well, I'm not an idiot. You think I'm going to spill everything to MacGregor without backing it up first? I plan to get evidence. But our van escapee is dead. I saw him die. Now I need to figure out what happened to him after that..." She pressed a palm to her eye socket and tried to shake off the ache in her head.

Danny moved to the doorway and took his keys from his pocket. "I've got to make an appearance in court this afternoon, so I have to run out, but I'll be back in a bit. Stay here and get some rest. I'll make us some dinner tonight when I get back. It's Friday. I'm off-duty all weekend. I'll help you get to the bottom of this. I promise."

When he walked out, Stella got up and watched from the front window as he climbed into the car and pulled out of the driveway. He waved and she raised her mug in response. Once he was out of sight, she took the cup of tea on a tour of the house as she searched for the telephone. She located it on the wall in the dining room. The phone book was nearby so she snatched it up, depositing herself at the dining room table and thumbing through the white pages until she found the Cs.

She ran her finger down the column of names. "Cabrera... Calhoun...Camello." She flipped the page. "Cameron. Robert." Her fingertip swept sideways to the address. It was the same one she recognized from the vehicle registration. She found a pencil and jotted the address on a scrap of paper, then noted the phone number as well. She checked the listings for an Elton Stenger but came up with nothing.

Next she located the Ls and searched the list until she came up with the name she was looking for. Longines, Malcolm. She got back up and reached for the phone, taking a moment to untangle the spiral cord that had formed a twisted knot beneath it. She dialed the seven numbers on the keypad, then stretched the phone cord so she could take a seat at the dining room table again.

The phone rang a dozen times. She was about to give up when someone picked up the receiver.

"Hello?" a male voice said.

"Yes, hello. Is this Malcolm Longines?"

"Speaking."

Stella leaned onto the table, her eyes focusing on the pavement out the window. "This is Special Agent Stella York from the FBI. We met yesterday at the scene of the fire downtown. Do you remember me?" There was a long pause on the other end of the line. "Hello? Are you there?" she asked.

"I'm afraid you must have the wrong number," he said.

"I also saw you at the impound lot," Stella added quickly, before he could hang up. "I didn't recognize you when I saw you yesterday, but you were the one on the scooter. Do you ride a pink scooter?"

"It's red," the man replied. "Not pink."

"Red," Stella replied. "Of course." She scrunched the phone cord in her hand. "But you were at the impound. You visited the van that crashed, didn't you? What were you doing there?"

"I don't know what you're talking about," Malcolm replied. "I have to go."

"I'm not going to report you," Stella blurted out. "I'm just looking for some answers. I'm investigating a prison escapee who came from the van whom I believe to be responsible for multiple deaths and fires in the city since. But there has been so much going on that makes no sense and I'm practically losing my mind over it. I *know* that you're connected somehow. I need your help to understand it. Can you please help me?"

The phone remained silent for several long seconds, but finally Malcolm responded. "You're only with the FBI? No one else?"

"Who else would I be with?" Stella asked.

"How old are you?" Malcolm asked.

"What has that got to do with anything?" Stella asked.

"How old?"

"Twenty-five."

"Right... you haven't met him yet," he replied. "I've seen your name in the files, but you're still too young."

"Haven't met who?" Stella was getting frustrated. The last thing she needed was more unanswered questions.

"I can help you, but we should talk in person."

"Where can I find you?" Stella asked.

"Do you know the softball fields off Sixteenth Street and Thirteenth Avenue? Woodlawn area?"

"No. But it's not far. I can find it."

"Meet me in half an hour. Field 5. Home dugout."

"Can you tell me why—"

But he hung up before she could finish.

Stella lowered the phone receiver and stared at it momentarily, then stood up to place it back on the wall.

She walked to the living room, picking up her holstered pistol from the coffee table. She took one last look around Danny's house, noting that she had left her mug of tea untouched on the kitchen table.

It would have to wait. She could rest later. It was time to get some answers.

9 / MALCOLM

The dugouts at the Woodlawn softball fields were simple slabs of concrete with metal benches. Being Florida, having actual subterranean seating for the ballfields would have been both impractical and an unnecessary expense. As far as locations for a meeting went, the benches were uncomfortable, the neighborhood questionable, and the scenery mundane. Stella found little to appreciate about the place and wondered why her rendezvous was taking place there.

She arrived several minutes early and scouted the area, but other than a few vagrants smoking in the picnic area, she found nothing of concern. She located the home dugout of field five and waited.

Malcolm Longines did nothing to conceal his arrival. The noise of his sun-faded scooter was audible several blocks away. He parked it on its kickstand near the curb and walked up the slight grade to the field. He was wearing acid-washed jeans and a black Robotech T-shirt. A messenger bag was slung over one shoulder. When he was a few yards away from the dugout, he stopped in the grass and assessed her. He took off his helmet.

"You don't look like an FBI agent," he said.

Stella crossed her arms. "Neither do you."

"I meant it as a compliment," the man said. "You look like . . . a nice person." The man was close to her age, with sharp eyes and a slight accent she hadn't noticed the night before. He walked a little closer. "I didn't have a chance to look at your identification the other day. Did you bring it?"

Stella reached into the pocket of her jacket and extracted her badge, holding it out so he could read it. "How about you? Who are you with?"

"I'm on my own at the moment," Malcolm replied. "But I work for a man who has . . . an interest in your case."

"So, you do know something about the prisoner van."

"I know it's not from around here," Malcolm replied. "And I know when it's from."

"When," she said. "Not where?" Stella studied his posture. He didn't stand like a crazy person. No fidgeting or nervous tics. There was a self-assurance to him that spoke of cold-reality. He looked a bit . . . geeky, for lack of a better word. She imagined him as someone who enjoyed hard data and not flights of fancy. "I've had a very strange few days. Things that are too odd to be coincidences. Then someone this morning started talking to me about time travel. I'm hoping I can count on you for more solid logic, because I didn't come all the way out here to indulge in a group fantasy or some kind of complex practical joke."

"I thought you came because you want to know the truth," Malcolm replied.

Stella put her badge away and recrossed her arms. "I'm here. I'm listening."

"I'm guessing you know the truth already," Malcolm said. "You must have seen the registration sticker on the license plate."

"The year twenty-ten?" Stella said. "Sure. But that didn't make me believe the van was really from the future."

Malcolm walked forward a few more steps and reached a hand into his bag.

Stella let her own palm rest on the pistol grip at her waist. She waited until Malcolm had removed a 4x6 photograph from the satchel and held it out to her before removing her hand from her gun. She took the photo.

"That's one of the men that was in the van the police impounded. "George Wallace. I expect you'll recognize him."

Stella studied the photograph. It showed the man she had last seen at the morgue, but he was alive in the photograph. It appeared to be a shot from work. Wallace was dressed in his guard uniform from the penitentiary.

"That's a photograph from roughly a week before the incident that sent Wallace back in time. June, 2009," Malcolm said.

"Two-thousand and nine?" Stella asked. "What's supposed to happen then?"

"It's a long story." Malcolm sighed. "But part of it happened right here." He pointed up.

Stella followed his gesture skyward, but saw nothing out of the ordinary overhead, just a bright Florida sky.

"The power line," Malcolm said, referencing the benign-looking cable she had failed to notice. "In two-thousand nine an experiment at a nearby lab facility goes badly and introduces a temporally unstable particle into the environment. It displaces over a dozen people through time. Many of them end up here."

"I don't understand. What's a temporally unstable particle?" Stella asked.

"It's a very special sort of particle," Malcolm added. "Once enough of them permeate an object or person, it can allow them to be displaced from the flow of time."

Stella studied the man's face. He was perfectly serious. "So time travel," she said. "Science fiction stuff."

"It won't become commonly used until the middle of the twenty-second century," Malcolm said, "but there are early pioneers that make use of it in the coming decades. This is an important era of history, temporally speaking. That's why I wanted to be involved."

"Even if I were to believe you, what you're talking about would have world-changing implications," Stella said. "Who else knows about it? Is it some kind of government project?"

Malcolm shook his head. "It's a private enterprise in this century. The regulatory body that oversees time travel has jurisdictional limits that don't precede the millennium. And they stick to prescribed timestreams. We're too remote."

"What's a timestream?" Stella asked.

"That's a longer explanation than I have time for," Malcom said. "But it means we aren't the only one."

"Only one of what?"

"Universes. Timelines. There are others. Parallel in some cases, other times completely unique."

"And you've seen this?" Stella asked. "Are you telling me you've been to other universes?"

"Not me," Malcolm said. "It's not my role. I'm a constant."

Stella eyed him skeptically. "So you're asking me to believe all of this time travel stuff even though you admit you've never done it? I imagine you don't have any proof either."

Malcolm shifted his bag on his shoulder and shrugged. "If you didn't already believe me, we wouldn't still be talking. I think you've seen enough to *know* that I'm telling the truth."

"This week has been weird. I'll give you that," Stella said. "But it's still a stretch."

"Why did you come then?" Malcolm asked. "On the phone you said you had questions." He took a few steps past her and sat down on the dugout bench. Stella followed him and sat as well, turning to face him.

"I saw something. Something that I know happened but that no one else can verify. It's like it got . . . erased."

She went on to describe the scene on the freeway and her return visit to find no evidence of the accident.

"You saw this accident happen before you ran into me at the lab?" Malcolm asked.

"Yes. Immediately before."

Malcolm looked pensive. "It's rare for someone to be consciously aware of a paradox, but it's possible that because you were so close to the epicenter of the change that your consciousness was able to perceive both of the diverging realities simultaneously."

"What are you talking about?" Stella asked.

"Yesterday, the building that was on fire was the epicenter of a temporal change. Someone came back in time and altered events on a scale that was initially merely paradoxical but then couldn't be contained. The timeline fractured, creating two separate realities. You and I are now sitting here talking in one reality, but in another, events have gone differently. It happens more often than we realize, but most people only feel the effects minimally—a brief feeling of deja vu is typically the worst of it. You had a more violent experience as your mind tried to reconcile the existence of two separate realities."

The weight of what she was involved in was settling into Stella's mind. As bizarre as his words sounded, she had to admit to herself that she believed him. Nothing else was coming close to explaining what she saw.

"Someone altered reality? Who?" she asked.

"I'm not at liberty to say," Malcom replied. "But events you witnessed were part of it. Elton Stenger was one of the time travelers involved. He was being transferred between prisons the night of the lab accident. The van hit a power pole and then jumped through time after being struck by the downed lines. He was the one who murdered the two victims in the van, and he was also responsible for several other murders. A law student and a prosecutor."

"The law office fire?" Stella recalled the night she had pursued Malcolm on the scooter and how she had encountered Danny outside the burning building. "Why? What was he after?" she asked.

"I don't have confirmation yet, but it seems the victims were both involved in his prosecution in 2009. The lawyer, Alan Waters, went on to be the judge that tried his case, and the law student was the future prosecutor for the state. The killings here in 1986 were revenge for the way he was convicted at trial. Perhaps he thought that if he killed them, then it would change his future."

"Will it?" Stella asked. "What happens now? If he killed the judge that sends him to prison in the future, how does he end up back here to kill them in the first place?"

"That's not how it works. It won't change anything in his original timeline," Malcolm said. "We are living in a new timeline now that has fractured away from the original version of events. Nothing he does will alter the future he came from, it will only create a new version of the events."

"I *saw* him die," Stella said. "He was killed on the freeway. Did his body disappear because he was from the future?"

Malcolm shook his head. "No. The accident you saw is part of another timestream now. Because it happened before the major break in the timestream at the lab, there was a brief window where both realities were overlapping. You were able to perceive the events of what would become an alternate reality for us now. But once you passed the point of the new fracture, the past no longer reflects what you saw. That's the paradox."

"I think I'm starting to understand why the whole thing made me dizzy," Stella muttered. "It's enough to make my head spin now."

"There is a lot we don't understand about paradoxical bubbles of time and how they behave prior to fractures in the timestream." Malcolm looked up at the power line again, as if he was reminiscing over a fond memory. "It's an ongoing area of research."

"You said you work for someone who knows about this? Is it someone I can talk to?"

Malcolm brushed a knuckle under his nose to scratch an itch, then looked across the street. "He's gone now. I had a message this morning. They got out of this timestream before the fracture. I'm supposed to shut everything down here and wait for further instructions as necessary."

"What do you mean? Where did they go?"

Malcolm shrugged. "They chose to follow the other branch of the timestream. I'm guessing they got out before the fracture so they wouldn't inadvertently duplicate themselves. They don't plan to stay active along this timestream anymore and don't want any extra versions of themselves created."

"You mean there are two different versions of us? Are you saying there's another me living a different life?"

"I wouldn't get too worked up about it," Malcolm said. "With as many time travelers as there are jumping around, and the fractal nature of the multiverse, there are probably a thousand other possible versions of you out there. Not that we'll ever meet them. For us, time will always feel like a boring straight line." He leaned over and snatched up a few blades of grass and started shredding them into smaller pieces.

"You don't sound like you're happy about it," Stella said. "Are you upset?"

"It doesn't matter," Malcolm said. "It's in my job description to stay put. Just thought maybe I'd get to at least stay in the active timeline. Bad luck, I guess."

"So some other version of you is going to keep working with

the time travelers? The one in the original timeline?" Stella asked.

"That's how it goes," Malcolm replied.

Stella tried to wrap her head around everything he was telling her—this universe of time travelers hidden from the rest of reality. At the very least it was a wildly imaginative fantasy he had constructed. If what he was saying was true, the repercussions for the world could be Earth-shattering.

"If you expect me to buy into this, I need to see something else as proof," Stella said. "Do you have any way to verify what you're saying?"

Malcom tossed away the bits of grass and let them flutter to the ground. "Doesn't matter now anyway. But what the hell." He reached into his bag and pulled out a small boxy object with a handle on it. It had a meter and a dial on its face. He twisted a power knob, then aimed the device at the bench they were sitting on. The meter jumped and began to oscillate. A second, digital indicator displayed a graph of some sort of wave. "There. That's a temporal frequency and it's got multiple layers now. See that?" He pointed to the graph.

"Is that supposed to mean something to me?" Stella asked.

"It's a temporal spectrometer," Malcom said. "It can tell when an object has been involved in a temporal event. This bench was where all the trouble started. If it weren't for this bench getting hit by that power line," he pointed skyward to the cable. "none of this would have turned out this way." He opened a compartment on the side of the box and popped out another smaller object that resembled a flashlight. He aimed that at the bench as well and pressed a button. Instead of illuminating the bench, a red light flashed on the device in his hand. "See? There's your proof for you. This bench has enough gravitized particles in it to infuse a Mack Truck. That's how big this temporal event was."

Stella picked her hand up from the bench, examining her palm and wondering if the particles he was talking about were somehow contagious. She wiped her hands on her pants and stood up. She studied her companion. "Look, I know this is all well and good for you, but it sounds like a bunch of gobbledygook to me. Is there any way you could show some of this to the Bureau? If I'm going to try to explain that my murder suspect is a time traveler, I'm going to need to be able to back it up with some scientific evidence. It sounds like you're the one who knows all about it. You could tell them what you told me and maybe we could close the case on this thing."

Malcolm stood up and put his tools back in his messenger bag. He adjusted it around to his hip. "Never going to happen," he said. "I only agreed to come meet you because I've seen your name in my boss's notes. You're listed as an ally with some people I trust. I don't care that you're with the FBI or what kind of case you guys need to solve. It doesn't matter now. The people with the answers you need are gone. I have no idea when they'll be back."

"Your boss said he knows me?" Stella asked. "What's his name? Have I met him?"

"You'll have to figure that out yourself," Malcolm said. "I'm not going to reveal his identity without his say so. I need to go." Malcolm picked up his helmet from the bench and began walking down the grassy embankment to his scooter.

Stella got up to pursue him. "Hold up a minute. There are still so many questions I need to ask you about this." She followed him down the embankment to the street.

Malcolm donned his helmet and climbed aboard the scooter, rocking it forward off its kickstand. "I probably shouldn't have told you as much as I have. You're going to try to get answers but let me save you the trouble. Soon, none of this will matter."

"I don't understand," Stella said. "This is the biggest case the Bureau has ever had. How can it not matter?"

"Because I'm going to clean it all up. I'll do my job. And tomorrow the world will go right back to thinking that there's no such thing as time travel."

10 / UNBELIEVABLE

STELLA HAD A LOT TO THINK ABOUT AS SHE WALKED THE streets of Saint Petersburg and made her way to the scene of the building fire on Ninth Street. The Crown Victoria had a parking ticket wedged under the driver's side windshield wiper. She tucked it into her pocket and stared up at the side of the burned building. Smoke and flames had stained the center windows black.

She glanced down the alleyway that ran alongside the building but wasn't tempted to return to the scene where she had passed out. Her head was aching enough already.

The streetlights were on by the time she made it back to Detective Briggs's house. The door was unlocked and when she entered the living room, she was met with the scent of baking bread. She slid out of her jacket and laid it on the arm of the couch. There were a couple of candles lit and the dining room table was set for two. She moved around the corner to the kitchen.

"Wondered when you'd make it back," Danny said, looking up from a pot of boiling water on the stove. "Hoped I'd see you."

Stella leaned against the kitchen door frame and stuck her hands in her pockets. "Didn't know you baked, Detective."

"I can manage the basics when the occasion calls for it." He wiped his hands on a towel. "Can I get you a glass of wine?"

"I could actually go for a beer," Stella said.

"Michelob or Budweiser?"

"Whatever's coldest."

Danny opened the refrigerator and pulled two silver cans from the back. He popped the top on one and handed it to Stella.

She waited until he opened his and then held hers aloft. "Here's to the weirdest case I've ever worked."

Danny tapped his can to hers and took a sip. "And let's hope it's the best inter-agency cooperation you've ever done. With any luck, we'll solve this thing."

Stella wiped a drop of condensation from her chin with the back of her hand. "So, I may have actually solved it tonight, but I doubt it's ever going to get resolved the way we think."

Danny pulled the bread from the oven and set it atop the stove to cool. "Solved it? What are you talking about?"

Stella gave him a brief account of her meeting with Malcolm in the park, watching Danny's expression as she did so. By the time she reached the part about the law student and prosecutor, his mouth was tight and he was shaking his head.

"Come on," Danny said. "He wants you to believe this? That he somehow knows the future? The thing about the van being an unknown model is strange, and I get that his story matches the registration sticker, but time travel? He's clearly got a screw loose. He watched that time car film too many times. The one from the billboard. Now he thinks he's Marty McFiggs."

"McFly," Stella said. "Yeah. I thought the same thing at first, but even though it's crazy, this *actually* explains what happened. You saw the undamaged power pole. It's because the van didn't hit the pole here. It hit it in the future! And the freeway? I know what I saw, Danny. That truck going under the overpass and knocking that guy into traffic wasn't something I can forget."

Danny shifted his feet and turned to dump the now boiled pasta into a colander. He sighed audibly.

"What?" Stella asked. "You know something else?"

"I don't know what I know," Danny replied.

"Where did you really go today?" Stella asked. "This afternoon. Were you looking into the accident?"

Danny turned to face her and leaned against the counter. "I talked to everyone I thought could have been involved. There was no accident on I-275 that night. Nobody had any idea what I was talking about."

"Then that's more proof that what this guy is saying is true! I know what I saw, and if it was some kind of shift in time that I was too close to like this guy says, then I have to believe it. It's the only explanation that matches up with what I know is true. Elton Stenger is dead."

Danny frowned. "Come on. People from different times? He expects you to believe that there are a bunch of other versions of us out there doing different things and people from the future running around offing people for things they haven't even done yet?"

"It's not science we understand now, but apparently someone will in 2009."

"But are you even listening to yourself? What kind of sense does that make? In some other version of our lives I made a choice to make you pizza instead of pasta and now there's an alternate reality where we're chewing pepperoni in the dining room?"

"I don't know how it works, Danny. I'm not an astrophysicist. But I know what happened to me and I saw the perp from the gas station fire get killed by an overpass on the freeway. I checked his body myself. If you don't believe me, I don't know what to tell you."

Danny took a few steps closer and took her hand. "I know you've been through a lot in the last couple of days. I'm not saying you're making it up, I just think there has to be another explanation."

"Like what? What else would explain what I saw?"

Danny rubbed her shoulder. "When those firefighters found you in the alley they said you might have suffered some smoke inhalation. What if something in that fire wasn't what we thought? What if you breathed in some kind of chemical?"

"It wasn't smoke inhalation," Stella said.

"But it could have happened while you were unconscious. It made you pass out, right? What if this whole car accident thing was a really vivid—"

"Hallucination?" Stella finished his sentence. She jerked her hand from his. "I *knew* you wouldn't believe me. I was stupid to think you would." She pushed him away and slid back through the doorway. "I'm not crazy, Danny."

"I'm not saying you're crazy," Danny replied. "I just think you might not be remembering things as accurately as you think. It happens all the time with victims of trauma. You know that. They said they found some strange stuff going on in that building once they put out the fire. If you were exposed to some unknown fumes from this place, who knows what it could have done to you?"

Stella walked to the couch and snatched up her jacket.

"Where are you going?" Danny asked. "Dinner's almost ready." He took a few steps toward her. "I thought tonight would be . . . romantic."

"You thought you'd make me dinner and take me to bed, and never mind that you think I'm crazy?"

"Well . . ."

"Goodbye, Danny." Stella flung the front door open and strode down the uneven walkway to the street. She was at the car by the time Danny reached the porch. She paused when she had the driver's door open, looking across the roof of the car to where

Danny stood illuminated by the porch light. He didn't pursue her. He lingered on the steps with his hand up and his mouth open. Stella locked eyes with him, and for a moment she thought he was going to say something, but then he slid his hands into his pockets and shut his mouth.

Stella sank into the seat of the Ford and started the engine.

She didn't look back as she pulled away.

By the time she reached the motel, her stomach was growling its displeasure. Would have been nice if the argument had come after dinner...

Why couldn't he open his mind? There was clearly more going on here than a normal case. Stella parked the Crown Victoria in the motel parking lot and stared at the faded door of her room.

She *saw* Stenger die. She wasn't crazy.

She got out of the car and made her way toward the doorway, searching for the motel key on her keychain. As she approached the door, someone spoke from behind her.

"You've had a call."

Stella spun around to find the hotel manager standing in the parking lot. She was a plump woman with square proportions and thick ankles that protruded beneath a floral mumu. The ankles terminated in wide feet stuffed into pink, fuzzy bunny slippers. She lifted a cigarette to her mouth, then exhaled the smoke from her nostrils as she spoke. "Here's your message." The manager held up a torn slip of paper.

Stella walked over and took the paper. The manager crossed one arm under her other elbow and held the cigarette aloft, observing.

Stella recognized the number of her field office even before she deciphered the name scrawled on the slip. Special Agent MacGregor.

"He sounded like he had a stick up his ass," the manager said.

"He always sounds like that."

The woman cocked her head. "You really an FBI Agent?"

Stella crumbled the piece of paper and stuffed it into her jacket pocket. "It's not as glamorous as it sounds."

"Never said it was." The woman took one last drag on the cigarette before dropping the stub to the pavement and squishing it beneath her slipper. "Checkout's at ten. No exceptions." She turned and shuffled her way back toward the office, letting out a rasping cough as she went.

Stella unlocked the door to her motel room to find that there had been no room service. The bed was still unmade. She deposited her jacket on the solitary chair and lifted the phone from its spot on the bedside table. She cradled the receiver in the crook of her neck and dialed the numbers as she carried the phone over to the table. It was late. There was likely no one left in the office, but she could at least leave a message with the night secretary.

The phone rang several times before a woman picked up. "Jacksonville Field Office."

"This is Special Agent Stella York." Stella went through the process of validating her identity and asked to leave a message for Special Agent MacGregor.

"I think Agent MacGregor is actually still in the office," the secretary said. "He passed by a few minutes ago. Do you want me to connect you?"

Stella hesitated briefly. "He's still working?"

"He's been in a meeting with SAC Renfroe, but I think they've been expecting your call. Hold please."

Stella waited for approximately twenty seconds before MacGregor picked up.

"York? What the hell have you been doing down there? I got a report you were in the hospital last night?"

Stella sighed. "I'm okay. They kept me overnight as a precaution."

"I've been on the phone with the Saint Petersburg chief of police. What's this about you claiming to have been in a car accident that never happened? According to him you've been keeping other officers from their duties and making them run down apparitions."

"What? Who told you that?" Stella said.

"Your handling of this case is making us the laughingstock of the station."

Stella clenched her jaw. What had Danny been saying today? The idea of him laughing it up with other officers at her expense made her nauseated. She sank into the chair.

"Renfroe's bringing you in and reassigning this case to another agent," MacGregor said. "Your ability to liaise with local law enforcement is clearly inadequate."

"I've finally gotten a major break," Stella objected. "If you pull me from the case now, you're never going to solve this thing."

"We have more experienced agents we can assign. Your performance has raised serious questions about your ability to work the field at all. I told you when we first started. You had one job. Don't make me look bad. You couldn't even manage that. Pack your bags and get on the road first thing. Renfroe expects you back in the office tomorrow with your report. Don't keep him waiting."

When Stella hung up the phone, it felt like the blood was draining from her body. She lacked the energy to even be angry.

To hell with this job.

To hell with MacGregor and Renfroe and the entire bureau.

Stella pulled her badge from her pocket and hurled it at the far wall. It thudded against the plaster and dropped to the dingy carpet.

She shouldn't be surprised. The entire system was rigged against her. They had assumed she'd fail before she even started.

Leaning forward, she buried her face in her hands.

She set her jaw. She wasn't going to cry. She wouldn't let herself sink to that level. If they broke her, that just meant they won.

With her eyes closed, images from the past few days ran wild through her mind. The crashed van that hadn't damaged the telephone pole. The young man, Ben, vanishing into thin air before Elton Stenger got hit by an overpass. Malcolm Longines and his blinking box analyzing a bench in a softball field dugout. It was all still there. It wasn't going away.

Stella pulled her hands from her face and placed them on her knees, pushing herself up from her chair. She walked the few feet to the carpet where her badge had fallen and picked it back up. The white edge of a photograph was protruding from behind the badge. She pulled it out and stared at it.

Her father's mustached face looked out at her from the black-and-white image, medals on his chest and a smile on his face.

"I'm letting you down, Dad," she muttered to the photograph. "I know you said I could be anything I set my mind to in this life, but I don't think you had an accurate count on all the assholes I'd get to deal with."

She stared at the photograph a little longer, then tucked it back into the fabric pocket behind her badge.

Stella stood in front of the hotel mirror and studied her own reflection. She looked tired. Defeated.

Without the job, what was she doing with her life?

She held the badge up to her reflection. Special Agent Stella York.

She lowered the badge again.

No. It didn't matter.

Badge or no badge, one way or another, she was going to figure this case out. She was going to do it for herself.

She just needed more time.

11 / ULTIMATUM

WHEN STELLA CHECKED OUT OF THE MOTEL IN THE morning, the manager barely said a word. The woman rasped out something about long distance phone charges and looked like she might be expecting an argument, but Stella merely signed the credit card receipt and left.

She might be leaving, but she wasn't done with St. Petersburg yet.

After she climbed into the Crown Victoria and started the engine, she reached into her jacket pocket and extracted the sheet of paper she had taken from Danny Briggs's house—the note containing the address for a Mr. Robert Cameron.

She studied the address one more time, then shifted into gear.

In less than fifteen minutes, Stella had located the old Spanish-style house and parked out front, taking a few minutes to size up the home. It was an unassuming neighborhood and quiet. Not the type of place one would expect to find members of a shadowy underworld conspiracy. But Stella had been wrong before.

She crossed the street and approached the house, lingering briefly on the porch. She knocked on the door and took a step back.

A dog barked.

Somewhere on the other side of the door, her knock had stirred up a commotion. The dog continued to bark and Stella heard several squawks that might be from birds. Finally a person opened the door, prying it open cautiously so as not to let the dog out. The red-haired man that greeted her was familiar. Carson.

"Uh, hi," he said when he finally extricated himself from the door and shut it behind him. He glanced down and caught sight of the pistol at her hip. "What's going on?"

Stella moved her jacket to cover the gun and pulled her badge from her pocket. "I'm Special Agent Stella York with the FBI. We met a few nights ago, do you remember?"

"Yeah, definitely," Carson replied. "Stella. Lover of mysteries. I'm sorry we didn't get to enjoy that beer together longer." He smiled at her. "FBI, huh? That's badass."

"It's not all it's cracked up to be."

"Maybe you need a Mulder to your Scully," Carson said.

Stella cocked her head. Sometimes it was like this group was speaking their own language. Carson seemed to sense her confusion.

"Sorry. Just a joke. You'll think it's funny in another ten years or so."

"Because it's a joke from the future?" Stella asked.

Carson crossed his arms and leaned against the doorframe. "I'm just messing around. What's going on?"

"I came here looking for your friend," Stella said. "Ben? The one you were singing with the other night? I was hoping to talk to him about some unusual circumstances he's been involved in."

"Yeah. I'm sure he'd love to help but you missed him. He left a few minutes ago."

"Will he be back later today?"

"Uh, no. They actually took off on a trip. Going to, um, can't quite remember the first stop. Boston maybe? But they won't be back for a while."

Stella frowned. "Is there a way I can contact him? Perhaps a phone number of somewhere he's staying?"

Carson chewed his lip. "Yeah, they won't be near a phone for a while either. It's sort of an off-the-grid kind of trip."

Off-the-grid in Boston? Stella sized him up. Despite the answers being unhelpful, he seemed to be open to talking.

"Are you familiar with a man named Malcolm Longines?"

Carson slipped his hands into his pockets. "Not really. But I think Ben chatted with him a few times, I haven't talked to him much."

"But you know who he is? Do you know who he works for?"

"Is this regarding something specific?" Carson asked. "Is Ben under investigation or something?"

Stella tried to smile reassuringly. "Nothing to worry about. Just trying to get a little help with a case I'm working on." She decided to try a different angle. "I need assistance solving an arson and murder case. Have you had any contact with a man named Elton Stenger?"

She saw a flicker of change in Carson's expression. To his credit, he didn't lie.

"I don't think that guy is going to be a problem anymore."

Stella's pulse quickened. "And why's that?"

"I don't know, I think I could take him. I'm not worried about it." He grinned. "Besides, you're going to catch him, right?"

Stella frowned. "So you think this Elton Stenger is still out there, but you don't think he's a threat?" She had hoped he would more directly confirm that Stenger was dead. "So, have you seen this guy lately? Stenger? In the last two days?"

"I'd rather not get into it." Carson fidgeted absentmindedly with the watch on his wrist.

Stella hadn't noticed the watch the last time she had met him, but it was a model she had never seen before, larger and more complex than any wristwatch she had ever come across.

"That's a nice watch."

"Thanks." Carson stopped fidgeting with the dials and put his hands behind his back.

"Do you mind if I ask where you were Thursday night?"

Carson smiled. "We were at the hospital that night. My friend's grandfather was ill. We went to visit him."

"This was Robert Cameron, the owner of this house?"

Carson nodded.

"And were you anywhere near Ninth Street and Fifteenth Avenue that night?" she asked.

"That's not far. Might have passed by."

"Do you know anything about the fire that started in a building near that address, or why your friend Ben might have been in the vicinity?"

"Wish I did. You'll have to ask him."

Stella was fairly certain he was lying now, but she wasn't positive. His expressions were difficult to read. Whatever he knew, she seemed to have reached the limits of his willingness to share. She reached into her pocket and pulled out a business card. "If you remember any more details that you think may be relevant to the events of that night, or if you have any more reasons to believe this Stenger guy is still a threat, give me a call, okay?"

"Happy to."

Stella took a few steps off the porch and then turned around. "What's your estimate for when your friend Ben might make it back to town? I'd like to speak with him too," Stella said.

"I wouldn't wait around on that," Carson replied. "It's going to be a few years."

"Years?"

"He's working on a project that's going to take a while. But if you feel like stopping back around 2009, I'm sure he'd be happy to chat with you." Carson winked at her and opened the front door. "See you later, Scully." Stella caught a glimpse of a happy-looking border collie peering around his legs before Carson disappeared inside.

Stella found herself staring at the house in curiosity.

Two-thousand and nine. That year kept popping up. She had a feeling it wouldn't be the last time.

When Stella sat down in Special Agent in Charge Renfroe's office, he already had her report in his hands.

She had typed it up the moment she was back in the office and suspected the ink might still be wet.

Special Agent MacGregor was in the room as well, looking as surly as she had last seen him. The days off hadn't seemed to help his demeanor.

"Let me see if I am getting this straight," Renfroe said, browsing over the pages. "You're trying to say that the incidents in this investigation are the result of an unknown group of persons . . . tampering with time?" He raised an eyebrow. "Is this really what I'm reading?"

"It sounds preposterous," Stella replied. "I thought so too, but when you look at individual elements of the case with that possibility in mind, the facts start to line up. I've spent a lot of time thinking about what I've seen, and I believe it warrants further investigation."

Renfroe scowled. "With that *possibility* in mind? What's next, we're supposed to consider alien abduction as a possible explanation for every missing person's case? Was Jimmy Hoffa caught up in the rapture? I can think of a lot of cases we could chalk up to the fantastical if we wanted to lose all credibility as an agency." He laid her report down and crossed his fingers on his desk. "I understand that you suffered a recent hospitalization, and I realize that as one of this office's first female agents, you may feel as though you are under a lot of pressure to prove yourself here. But that does not mean we are going to cast off reality in the course of an investigation simply so that you can gain attention. I suggest that you seriously consider the future path of your career with the FBI as you frame your response."

Stella scooted forward on her chair. "Sir, I can assure you that no part of this report is an attempt to gain attention for myself. I believe that there is something worth investigating here. I understand that my career in this office has been short so far, but can you recall ever having a case with this many paradoxical irregularities?" She gestured southward. "There is a man in the St. Petersburg morgue that appears to be a genetic clone of George Wallace, or, as has been suggested, he *is* George Wallace from the year 2009. Everything about this case is irregular, right down to the victims. In order to resolve this, we are going to have to look into all the facts, and some of those facts are going to seem fantastical until we finish the investigation and find out the truth."

Renfroe held up her report. "And you plan to defend your story of having witnessed a fatal traffic accident on Interstate 275 that killed our perpetrator, despite the fact that no one can corroborate your account?"

Stella hesitated only briefly. "According to one of my sources, that was possibly a glimpse of an alternate timeline, but I know what I saw."

Renfroe sighed and laid the report back on the desk. "Let me make things very clear for you, Miss York. You are going to be reassigned. Special Agent MacGregor will be assisted by another agent and you will have nothing more to do with this case, is that understood?"

Stella wanted to object but kept her mouth shut.

"I suggest you take the rest of the day off. When you come in on Monday, we'll determine where this office will make use of your talents. You'll turn in any remaining information on the case to Agent MacGregor."

Renfroe stood, and Stella rose from her chair as well. She made her way over to the door. She paused with her fingers on the doorknob and looked at MacGregor. "Well, you got what you wished for, Bart. Now you can prove how well you can solve the case without me slowing you down."

"You think I don't know? With another partner, I'll have it done in a week."

"We'll see." Stella opened the door and stepped through, closing it behind her.

THIRTEEN YEARS LATER.

"IT DOESN'T MATTER that it's your personal copy of the video," Stella said into the phone. "It's not licensed for commercial use." She leaned back in her chair and checked the clock on the wall.

Still another twenty-five minutes to go.

"Yes, I get that complaint a lot. It's not the type of situation we can investigate unless we have evidence of an actual crime."

The woman on the other end of the phone continued to ramble.

"Yes, ma'am, I understand that you're upset that he taped over your shows but that's the danger of VHS tapes. I don't know if you know, but if you break off the little tab on the label edge he won't be able to . . . No. I'm sorry. We can't arrest your husband for that."

She placed her head into her palm and leaned against her desk. "You can certainly stay on the lookout for anything else suspicious. Yes, ma'am. Thanks for your call."

She hung up the phone and checked the clock again. Twenty-three minutes to go.

Stella pivoted in her chair and faced her computer again. A colorful memo was pinned to the bulletin board on the wall behind it. ARE YOU READY FOR Y2K? BACK UP YOUR FILES!

Stella browsed through her latest email until the phone rang again. She looked up at the clock. Damn. Still had to take it.

She lifted the receiver. "FBI Las Vegas Office. This is Special Agent Stella York. How may I help you?"

"Hi, Stella. It's Detective Danny Briggs. It's been a long time."

Stella sat up straight in her chair.

Danny Briggs?

"Uh hello, Danny. What's . . . Why are you calling me?"

"Hey, I know we didn't leave things on the best of terms all those years ago, but something's come up with the case we were working on together and I thought I should call you."

A few agents walked by chatting and Stella waited until they had passed before speaking again. "You're talking about the St. Petersburg van murders?"

"There's been a development. Do you have a minute?"

"Um, sure. But it's not one of my cases anymore, Danny. I'm not even in Florida. I'm out west in Las Vegas now."

"I know. I'm not there either. I moved out to California a few years ago. But I ran into a connection to the case out here and I think you should hear about it."

Stella settled back in her chair. "What's going on?"

"It has to do with a recent murder. It happened here in L.A. a couple days ago. It's a high profile homicide and they want answers quickly. They pulled me in because they found out I had some prior experience with the case. Unfortunately we don't have a lot to go on."

"Who's the victim?"

"His name's Carson Bradley. You might have heard of him.

He was a big shot music and film producer out in Hollywood. Produced some mega-star artists."

"I do know him," Stella said, her mind flashing back to decade-old memories. "I met him in St. Petersburg. He's been murdered?"

"A few days ago. Someone kidnapped Bradley's girlfriend, and when he tried to deliver the ransom, he ended up dead. The L.A. Police Department was able to get some prints from the house—the scene of the abduction, and they matched some we had on file from the van murders in St. Petersburg. I know you always swore that guy was dead, but I think you should know, they matched the record we have for an Elton Stenger. Local PD tracked him down in Gainesville yesterday. They've arrested him for the murder."

Stella ran a quick search of the system for an update on Elton Stenger, and waited for the page to load. A few seconds later, a mugshot appeared. Something was definitely wrong.

"I know he's in the system now, Danny, but that can't be the same guy. He had to be close to forty when he burned those buildings in St. Petersburg." She checked the date of birth on the computer record. "This guy would have been seventeen at the time."

"I know it doesn't add up," Danny said. "That's one of the reasons I wanted to call you."

Stella frowned. "So you can have a good laugh seeing me try to convince the Bureau to reopen the investigation? No thanks, Danny. It's not my problem now."

The detective sighed audibly on the other end of the phone. "Listen, I also called because I wanted to tell you that I was wrong to write off your experience back then," he said. "I should have believed you years ago, but I was an idiot. I'm sorry."

Stella shifted the phone to her other ear. "Would have been

nice to hear that at the time, but . . . thanks. What made you change your mind?"

"When I saw this guy's name come up again, it set me thinking about the dead ends we had run into on the case before. You remember the drivers of the van that we examined at the morgue? One looked just like his dopplëganger, and one was a John Doe?"

"Um, yeah. Wallace, right? Something Wallace?"

"Right. But I got to thinking about the other guy, the one we couldn't ID. I decided to run his prints through the system again and this time I got a hit. An eighteen year old guy named Brian Halpert just started work in the prison system. I got my hands on a photo and it's the same kid. Still younger than when we saw him by about ten years, but it's him. So if he goes back in time at the age we saw him, that would be around—"

"Two thousand and nine," Stella said.

"I've tried to come up with any other explanations, but yours is the only one that makes any sense. This shit has to be some kind of time travel."

"Hope you aren't staking your career on it. I can tell you how that turns out."

"I'm keeping my thoughts to myself for now, but after I told the department here about your investigation, they wanted me to reach out to you. And it's not just our personal history with the case that made me want to call. There was something at the scene too."

"What?"

"The victim—Carson Bradley. He had an old business card in his wallet from the FBI. A business card with your name on it. Phone records show he tried to call, too, right before he went off looking for the kidnapper."

Stella's gut clenched. "He tried calling for help?"

"I don't know why he called, but he did. Didn't get the right office, since you moved, and he apparently didn't get word on how to reach you. I just figured you should know. And I feel the same way you do about the Elton Stenger from Gainesville. The Department is set on prosecuting him, but I can't help thinking we have the wrong guy. I think whoever killed Carson Bradley is still out there."

Stella checked the area around her desk to see if anyone was paying attention, then rolled open her desk drawer as far as it could go, reaching into the back for a tattered file folder she hadn't handled in months. She laid it on her desk and rested a hand on it. Did she really want to reopen this chapter of her life? Her fist clenched, almost involuntarily, but then she opened her palm and rested it atop the file.

"If I get involved in this again, are you going to have my back?" she said.

"There's no way I'm cracking this without you," Danny replied. "I hope you can forgive me."

Stella chewed her cheek. "I guess I'll have plenty of time to think about it. I'm taking a drive tonight."

13 / CARSON

Las Vegas to Los Angeles was a four hour drive on a good day. It was a lot of time for introspection, and dredging up the emotions of the case.

St. Petersburg had been a long time ago. Two office transfers. A rocky marriage. A nasty divorce. It felt like several lifetimes had passed since then. Despite the fallout from her time assisting the Tampa office, she'd salvaged her career in the Bureau. She hadn't talked about her experience in St. Petersburg for over a decade, but she still kept the file. And over the years it had grown.

She flipped the folder open on the passenger seat next to her as she drove.

There had been new snippets added. News articles. Missing persons reports. It was hard to know what was relevant anymore, but Stella had never been able to let the case out of her mind. On one side of the folder she'd even stapled a publicity photo of TV Special Agent Dana Scully from the X-Files. One more piece in the puzzle.

There had been other killings over the years. Fires. Chewed match sticks found at crime scenes. It was hard to tell how many were connected.

She picked up a faded newspaper clipping from the pile.

NOTED SCIENTIST MISSING.

The article spoke of a scientist named Dr. Harold Quickly who had disappeared from a lab in St. Petersburg a few years ago. He was supposed to be working on a new theory to explain time. Last seen at the Temporal Studies Society. An employee records search listed a Malcolm Longines there as well. Malcolm Longines who said he had a boss who disappeared from another timeline in 1986.

She no longer believed in coincidences.

There were other articles too. Odd bits of news about Carson Bradley and his meteoric career in the entertainment industry. His talents as an artist were respectable, but his success as a writer and producer had been far superior. No less than fifteen of the albums he produced had hit number one on the charts. He dabbled in screenwriting for Hollywood too, producing several blockbuster franchises that critics had called visionary. In one red-carpet photo, he grinned back at the camera with his girlfriend, Jessica Poist, on his arm. The happy couple apparently had no idea what was coming.

Detective Danny Briggs still looked good. The intervening decade had added a few pounds and his hairline had crept back, but his brilliant blue eyes still had the same way of crinkling at the corners when he smiled at her. And he was holding a case file of his own.

It was nearing midnight. Far too late for a rendezvous for evidence collecting, but he was there. Stella appreciated the effort.

"You'll have to thank your wife for sparing you tonight, detective. I'm sure you have other places you could be."

He hooked his thumb on his pocket. "She gets thanked every month with an alimony check these days. We split up last year."

"I'm sorry to hear that."

And she was sorry. The pain of her own divorce wasn't something she'd wish on anyone.

Danny shrugged and scratched at the back of his neck. "Seems like it's just part of this job. No one ever gets all of us, do they?"

"You ever tell her the truth about this case?"

Danny shook his head. "You?"

"Yeah, actually. Not that it was a good idea."

Stella recalled the arguments with her ex-husband about her "delusion" after she had finally opened up to him. To be fair, he had played along with the idea of time travel existing in the beginning—put it down as a harmless eccentricity. He made occasional jokes but mostly left it alone. It was only when he had discovered the growing files she kept at home and the years of research she had done that he questioned her sanity.

"I think everyone has a case that never lets them go," Danny said. He raised his own file folder.

"Are you officially on the case?" Stella asked.

"My chief didn't want me anywhere near it. Not my job. But I called in a few favors and he said as long as I don't get in the way I'm all right. How about you? You tell the feds in Vegas you were coming out?"

"I'm on vacation," Stella said. "Not that they'll ask. I've been left to die a slow death in the video fraud department."

"Ouch. Hunting down porn pirates?"

"That would probably be a step up." Stella gestured toward the little house they were parked in front of. "So, you still have the search warrant for this place?"

The detective checked his watch. "We actually only have a few minutes left on it, but since you're in town I wanted you to see it."

He stooped and picked up something from the ground. "Oh

yeah. Found at least a dozen of these laying around out here too." He held up the item for Stella's inspection. It was a matchstick with several teeth marks at one end.

"Like the van," Stella said.

Danny flicked away the matchstick and gestured with the file folder toward the door. "After you."

They walked up the steps of the bungalow and Danny fished the key from the lockbox. "Stenger had this place as a short term rental. Deal was done over the phone though. Landlady never saw him in person."

"She's cooperating with the investigation?"

"Wanted us to keep her out of the papers, which we did. Can't blame her."

The door swung open. Stella found herself inside a cozy, unassuming vacation rental. The furniture was slightly dated but clean and unremarkable. She wandered into the living area.

"We took pictures of everything when we first got here, lifted a few solid prints. We did find a couple of strange things."

"Like what?"

"For one, the fridge is stocked with enough food and beer to last a month. But according to the landlady, he only rented the house for two weeks."

"So he was planning on entertaining guests?"

"I suppose he could have wildly overestimated what the Poist girl would eat while he held her hostage. But I'm guessing maybe he thought it would take longer than it did to off Carson Bradley. The creepy thing was that he had a spread of news articles set up over here on the desk. Some about himself. The rest were about famous serial killers." The detective laid the file folder on the desk and opened it.

Stella looked it over and examined the photos he had taken. "Dahmer, The Nightstalker, The Zodiac Killer. This is a regular Who's Who. You're thinking he has idols?"

"Or competition," Danny said.

Stella flipped through a few more photos from the night the evidence was collected, browsing the shots as she walked the various rooms. "So he had Jessica Poist tied up in the back bedroom. Carson Bradley comes to rescue her, most likely with some kind of ransom to trade. The exchange goes badly and somehow Carson gets killed?"

"The girl never saw the action unfold. She was blindfolded as well as tied up in the other room. Says she heard some shouts from Bradley so she starts screaming. She hears a struggle. She knocks the chair over and ultimately gets herself loose, but by then Bradley is dead and Stenger is gone. She's the one who called for police."

"We have any idea what Stenger wanted as a ransom demand?"

"Bradley never contacted the authorities about the kidnapping. Maybe he had something to hide and this guy was blackmailing him. Hard to say. All we know is it went badly for him when he got here."

Stella studied the photos of the initial crime scene, then scanned the main room again, trying to get a feel for how it looked at the time. Carson's body was gone and the room had already been cleared of whatever evidence the investigators thought relevant. After a brief tour of the main features, she donned a pair of rubber gloves and started poking around more thoroughly. Danny browsed the scene as well. It was only when Stella had dropped to her knees to peer under the recliner that he seemed to fidget. "The team already had a pretty good look at the room."

"I'm not saying they didn't," Stella replied. "But it never hurts to have a second one." She clicked on her flashlight and scanned the floor. Finding nothing but dust bunnies, she shuffled a few feet to the couch and repeated the process.

"We've already got the murder weapon."

Stella's light illuminated a rounded shape behind a leg of the sofa. She moved around the side and nudged the coffee table aside to retrieve the object. When she pulled it loose, she discovered it was a miscellaneous knob from a piece of furniture. She was vaguely disappointed. She dropped it into an evidence bag anyway.

"Death by door knob?" Danny quipped.

Stella set the evidence bag on the desk and resumed her perusal of the room's nooks and crannies. After a few minutes, she straightened up and poked her head into the other rooms. Finally she returned to Danny. "What's it from?"

Danny cocked his head quizzically. "What's what from?"

"That knob," Stella said. "It doesn't match any of the furniture." She wandered back into the kitchen and double-checked the cabinets.

Danny picked up the evidence bag with the loose knob in it. "Maybe it was from a piece the landlord no longer has." He studied the metallic finish on the knob. "Maybe I should check it for prints though, just in case. Looks like there might be a pretty clear partial on this side."

The digital clock on the oven changed from 11:59 to 12:00.

Stella slowly removed her gloves as Danny led the way toward the door. "We have any clue where Stenger has been all this time?" she asked. "How's he been able to stay off the radar since St. Petersburg?"

"I'm hoping we find out when we ask him," Danny replied. He held the door for her. "Assuming he ever shows his face again."

Stella buttoned her jacket. "I have some ideas on how to arrange that."

. . .

The L.A. County Coroner was in early the next morning but Stella was already waiting for him in the parking lot with a second cup of coffee.

"You must be the agent Detective Briggs told me about." The coroner had a friendly face partially obscured by a graying mustache. He wore a tan windbreaker over his alligator polo. He cautiously accepted the extra coffee from Stella. "This from the gas station?"

"No. Maria's Bakery. On Marengo Street."

The coroner's eyebrows lifted and he took an enthusiastic sip. "Oh, okay then." He extended a hand. "Mel Odenkirk."

"Stella York."

He let her inside the employee entrance and they traversed the hallways to the stairs.

"I've been coming in early to stay ahead of the press. Every time we get a celebrity death around here, they hang around like buzzards. But I hear you knew the deceased before he got famous?"

"We were acquainted briefly in St. Petersburg, Florida, but that was years ago."

"I have an old aunt who lives near there. She calls it 'God's waiting room.'"

"They do have a lot of seniors." Stella followed Mel to his office. "What can you tell me about the homicide? I heard you examined him."

"Some of my staff did. I only got involved due to all the press scrutiny. But I do have copies of the photographs from the autopsy." He rummaged through items on his desk and came up with a folder. "You're welcome to read the report."

Stella thumbed through the file, pausing at the description of the wounds the victim had received. "You mention in here that his left wrist got scratched up. Some sort of defensive wound?"

"No. Best we can tell, that happened after he had already been killed. We think the killer had trouble getting something off his wrist. We assume it must have been an expensive watch he wanted. Makes sense with as much money as Bradley was worth."

The Nokia ringtone sounded from Stella's jacket pocket. When she retrieved the phone and answered it, Danny Briggs was on the other end of the line.

"Hey, I got the results back on that partial fingerprint from the furniture knob from last night. Guess who they match?"

Stella mouthed a silent 'thank you' to Odenkirk, then retreated to the hallway before returning her attention to the phone.

"Don't tell me it was Stenger."

"Nope. Carson Bradley."

"Weird," Stella muttered. "So what, he brought it from home and somehow dropped it there? Was anything stolen from his home or from his person?"

"Not that we know of. Unless you count the kidnapping of the girlfriend."

"What about his wallet and car keys? That sort of thing."

"All still on him. Good bit of cash in there too."

"So if the killer wasn't after money, why did he take the watch?"

Danny exhaled loudly into the other end of the phone. "Beats me. It had to be personal. Some kind of vendetta and the watch was part of it."

The watch.

Was it possible that it was the same watch Carson had been wearing a decade ago?

When she got back to the car, Stella checked the still photos taken from the video surveillance tapes that Danny had given her. The man caught in the frame was grainy and poorly defined, but definitely Elton Stenger. Even with the grainy shot, she knew it wasn't the guy they had arrested in Florida.

Elton Stenger was still alive, still on the loose, and Carson Bradley showed up to meet him with a furniture knob.

"What did his girlfriend say when she got picked up? Did she visually identify her kidnapper?"

"I wasn't part of that interview. I only know what we have in the report."

"I need to talk to the girlfriend. She's the only one who made direct contact with Stenger."

There was a clattering of clipboards on his desk. "She moved in with a friend in the valley after the incident. I think I have the address. Don't know if she'll want to talk though. From what I hear, she's a bit of a mess."

"Can you blame her?"

"I'll get you that address."

STELLA PRESSED the button of the call box of the Beverly Hills Luxury Apartments but after three attempts and subsequent waiting, decided no one was home. It was only when she had turned to walk away that the speaker crackled.

"What do you want?"

Stella turned back toward the door. "Jessica? I'm Special Agent Stella York from the FBI. I just wanted to talk for a few minutes."

"I told them I was done talking to cops."

"I knew him. I knew Carson. I'm the one he tried to call."

After a long few seconds, the door buzzed.

It was three flights up, but when she reached the apartment, the door was cracked. She pressed on it until it swung open, then stepped inside.

The place smelled of patchouli and the lingering scent of pot smoke.

She found Jessica in the living room, sunk into one corner of a sagging, faux leather couch. The woman was only in her late twenties, with her blonde hair styled to match the latest of Jennifer Aniston's "Rachel" hairdos.

"That smell isn't from me," she said, as soon as Stella had entered the room. "Some people just left."

"I'm not DEA," Stella said. "You mind if I sit?"

Jessica made no objection, so Stella perched on a nearby ottoman.

"I'm very sorry for your loss, Jessica. For the brief time I knew him, Carson seemed like a good guy."

Jessica chewed her lip and fidgeted with a strand of her hair. "He was unlike anybody I ever knew."

Stella leaned forward to rest her elbows on her knees. "Can I ask you about the watch? The one that was stolen?"

"I already told the cops. I don't know how much it was worth."

"That's not what I want to know," Stella said. "I'm more interested in what it could do."

Jessica's eyes narrowed. "What are you talking about?"

"I've seen that watch, Jessica. I know it wasn't just a trinket that someone would have tried to resell. Did Carson tell you anything about what it was for? You were together for quite a while. I'm guessing he trusted you with his secret."

Jessica was studying her intently now, trying to read the truth in her face. Stella met her gaze and didn't look away.

"He told me some of it."

Yes. Now she was getting somewhere.

Stella resisted the urge to press for more and instead let the silence do the questioning.

Jessica fidgeted with a bit of loose thread on the armrest

stitching. "I didn't get to go with him or anything, but he told me about where he got the songs, and . . . some of the money. It's not like anything he did was illegal."

Stella shot for her center target. "Was the watch that was stolen off his wrist what let him travel in time?"

Jessica chewed her lip again, possibly waiting for a follow-up joke or dismissive explanation. When none came, she nodded. She crossed her arms and tucked her legs in closer, balling herself up in the corner of the couch. "I knew no one would have believed me if I told them what it really was."

"I believe you. And I get why you're so scared that Elton Stenger has it," Stella concluded.

"He's a psycho crazy person," Jessica said. "And there's nothing the cops can do to catch him. They think he's caught already."

"I don't."

Jessica met her stare again. "But you're one person. No one else will ever believe you. How are you going to stop him?"

"I've seen someone do it before. We can do it again. But, Jessica, I'm going to need your help."

14 / JESSICA

Entrance to Carson Bradley's Bel Air mansion involved an electronic key pad and a security gate. Jessica typed the six digits without even having to look.

The grounds of the sprawling Tudor-style mansion were gorgeous and utterly silent, secluded from the road by high brick walls and an even higher barrier of trees.

Stella had been among wealthy people before, but had never been to a mansion with this much celebrity history. Before Carson had purchased the luxury home, it had apparently belonged to Tom Jones, and Dean Martin before that.

Jessica parked the convertible BMW near a fountain where sun bleached stone lions spit water from their mouths into a circular pool. Once she shut the car off, she simply stared out the windshield at the ivy-covered facade. From the passenger seat, Stella had no trouble reading her body language.

"I know it can be stressful coming back to a place like this after a trauma. Take your time."

Jessica clenched her jaw and opened the door. Stella joined her around the front of the car and the two of them approached the mansion together. Jessica exhaled audibly, then kept her head down, leading the way through the front door with a look of stark determination on her face.

Stella didn't know Carson Bradley well, but she was still surprised by the interior of the mansion. Wood floors were mirrored by polished wood beams, and in some rooms, intricately carved ceilings. The elaborate moulding on the walls and fancy chandeliers spoke of a bygone era of opulence. It seemed a far cry from the carefree young man she had seen belting out karaoke tunes in a St. Petersburg bar.

Jessica was out of place here too, like she had been playing the role of a wealthy celebrity's girlfriend but now that Carson was gone, she no longer wanted to keep the act up. She seemed to be shrinking inward as if the pressure of being inside the mansion was causing her own exterior to crumble.

It wasn't until they entered the library that Jessica seemed to relax. "It's this way."

Jessica walked around a mammoth desk, then moved to the mantle of the fireplace. A series of trophies stood sentinel atop it.

Stella's eyes widened. Was that a Grammy?

Jessica took hold of one of the awards and carefully twisted the base.

To the right of the fireplace, a cleverly disguised bookcase door slid open to reveal a hidden room. Jessica gestured for Stella to follow.

"The secrets just keep coming," Stella muttered as she stepped inside.

The room was roughly fifteen feet square and covered in wall-to-wall shelves that were loaded with a wild assortment of strange knickknacks. Metal figurines, components from lamps, and loose bricks sat beside old shoes, doorknobs, and bits of plumbing pipe. It had the clutter of an antique store but with the organization of an office supply closet. Each strange and seemingly unrelated item was categorized on a shelf, and each shelf held dates and other letter-number combinations that she didn't understand.

The object that caught her eye, however, was a metal stand in the center of the room. The single steel pole rose to about the height of her waist before culminating in a shallow, wire basket. Inside the basket, erected on its end, sat a metal cabinet knob that was an exact match to the one she had found under the couch in the rental house.

"What on earth is that doing here?" She immediately strode over to the basket and picked up the knob.

It was identical.

"He called them anchors," Jessica said. "He always carried something like that in his pocket. He said it was in case he needed a quick exit."

Stella noted a hardbound journal that was laid open on a neighboring countertop. She moved to examine it and found it filled with entries in rowed columns. Time of departure. Location of departure. Location of arrival. Time of arrival. There were other places to note changes in time zones and descriptions of the "anchors" being used. Stella flipped back through the last few pages. The times listed were mostly close together, sometimes only a matter of hours or minutes. But they went back years.

She got a chill up her spine.

It was real, and Carson had been doing it.

Time travel.

"He called this his vault," Jessica said. "He liked the play on words. Because he said he was vaulting across time. Sometimes he'd be gone for weeks."

"You're saying this is the actual room he used to jump through time?"

"I know. Seems like it ought to be bigger. In the movies they always have giant machines and stuff. He said it wasn't like that in real life."

"How *does* it work?"

"It doesn't work at all for normal people. You have to be a time traveler. Carson said there's a special particle in them that regular people don't have. It's why he could never take me with him. It's why I can't go back and–" Her breath caught and she covered her mouth with her hand.

"I didn't mean to upset you," Stella said. "I'm sorry. I know this must be difficult."

"It's so frustrating, you know?" Jessica held the back of her hand to her nose. "He had this amazing ability and he came to save me, and I can't do anything to go back and save *him*."

Stella rested a hand on the young woman's shoulder, caressing it gently.

"I'm okay." Jessica composed herself, wiping at her eyes. "This is just hard."

"This is asking a lot of you. I get that. But if you can help me to understand how this works, I'll be better prepared for catching this guy. Is there anything else you can tell me? Did Carson by chance have more than one of those special watches? Maybe one I could look at?"

Jessica shook her head. "There was only one chronometer. That's what he called it. But he did have another thing that he said was important. She moved to the countertop and opened the door of a device that vaguely resembled a microwave. "Sometimes he had me put clothes and stuff in here for him. He said he had to treat all the things he took with him with these special particles before he went anywhere, otherwise they wouldn't make the trip. He called it a gravitizer." She moved to a drawer and looked inside. "And he had another thing called a degravitizer for taking them back out of stuff." She opened a second drawer. "Here it is." She removed a box with a gauge on it and opened the side to reveal a smaller cylindrical device that vaguely resembled a flashlight.

"I think I've seen one of those before," Stella said, recalling her rendezvous with Malcolm Longines at the ball fields in St. Pete. This was the same thing he had used to try to convince her of the truth of time travel. "You have any idea where he got this stuff?"

"He said it was from old friends."

Stella studied the gravitizer device. "You said in your report to the police that while Stenger had you hostage, he kept ranting about how he wanted to be the 'only one.' Is that true?"

"Yeah. It's all he wanted to talk about. How he was going to be famous again, and everyone would fear his name. And he said he had to be the only time traveler."

"There was another bit in your account of that night. Something about him wanting to 'get even with someone quickly.'"

"Yeah. But I don't know who he was talking about. He never said the person's name."

"I think maybe he did." Stella reached into her file of newspaper clippings and extracted the one about the missing St. Petersburg scientist. "I know what you thought you heard, but is there a chance that 'Quickly' was actually the name of the person he was talking about?"

She held out the article for Jessica to read.

Jessica scanned the caption of the black-and-white photo. "Doctor Harold Quickly?"

"I think this man is somehow connected with Carson's travels in time," Stella said.

"I don't know. I've never met him."

Jessica handed the photo back. "If this Quickly guy is involved, how does that help us?"

"I'm not sure. I do have an idea about how to flush Elton Stenger out of hiding. But before we do that, I'm going to need you to tell me everything you know about that watch."

15 / STENGER

"This has to be the silliest idea I've ever heard of," Danny said. He folded the newspaper in half and reread the classified ad at the bottom of the page.

"We know he reads the L.A. Times," Stella replied. "You have a better way to get a hold of him?"

Danny frowned. "It's ridiculous." He paced across the living room rug of his rented condo.

"Elton Stenger won't think so." She was seated at his dining room table, their collected files spread out in front of her.

Danny squinted slightly as he read the small newsprint. "Wanted: Fellow time traveler to join me in expedition to the past. I can provide a chronometer and de . . gravi . . . tizer?" He lowered the paper and stared at her. "You know how many whack jobs you're going to get responding to this?"

"They've already started calling. Doesn't matter. Stenger is obsessed with being the only time traveler, which means he'll want to find out who this person is. He'll make the rendezvous."

"From a classified article using made up words."

"To real time travelers, they aren't made up."

"He'll know it's a setup. No way he shows."

"Since we've been on this case, how many people other than you and I actually believed time travel was possible?"

"Zero."

"So I'm guessing no one ever believed Stenger either, meaning, in his mind, the likelihood of law enforcement showing up should be low."

"You have no idea what other time travelers he's run into. He killed Carson Bradley, but how do we know he was the first? There may be any number of these people. Or who's to say someone worse doesn't show up?"

"But if he's out to get them—and we know he is—he'll at least want a look at who shows up too. Whoever else shows up, Stenger will be there."

Danny shook his head. "I don't know. Have you thought hard about what you're getting into? If this is legit, and there really are time travelers going around changing the past, how do we compete with that? Is that even in our job description?"

Stella fixed him with a hard stare. "Come on, Danny. I know you've been on the job a long time, but you have to want to bring this guy down. After all we've been through to catch him, you want to walk away now?"

Danny clenched his jaw as he considered her. "Okay. But we're at least going to run this through official channels. If you're going to meet up with this guy, we need backup. The chief is already going to tear me a new one for letting you do this much without consulting the leads on the case. I'm hoping I can smooth it over and get us the support we need. Promise me you won't try to rendezvous with this guy on your own."

"I'd love all the backup I can get."

"So let's be clear. You're promising you won't try to take this guy down on your own. I need to hear you say it."

Stella held up three fingers. "Scout's honor." She collected her files and rose from her chair. "It's getting late. I ought to get back to my hotel. We've still got a lot of work to do."

Danny sighed and nodded. He walked with her toward the door and reached to open it for her. He paused with his hand resting on the doorknob. "You know, I don't regret too many things in my life, but I do regret never getting that date night with you all those years ago."

Stella crossed her arms over the files she was carrying. She studied his face. His eyes were still kind and smiling. He still looked good. "Yeah. I regret that too."

"Vegas isn't that far a drive. Maybe when all this is over I can buy you dinner?"

"I think I'd like that."

Danny opened the door, but kept his eyes locked to hers.

Stella took a step closer, then leaned forward and gently kissed his cheek, just brushing the corner of his mouth. "Goodnight, Danny."

She turned and descended the steps of his condo, only turning back when she reached the sidewalk. He waved from his doorway. She smiled and headed for the parking lot, walking a little bit lighter in her shoes.

She pulled her phone from her pocket as she walked and noted that the proxy number she had published in the newspaper had already routed another dozen replies to her voicemail. She pressed the play button and cradled the phone in her neck as she fished the car keys from her pocketbook.

"Hey. This the time traveler? How much you want to go back and shoot my ex-wife before—"

Stella muttered a curse, then quickly hit the delete button before selecting the next message. She opened the car door and slid into the driver's seat, tossing her file folders to the passenger side. For some reason the dome light hadn't come on.

She located the ignition switch in the semi-darkness and had just put the phone back to her ear when the cold metal pressed into her neck.

"Drop the phone. Then put your hands up real slow."

An immediate chill went down Stella's spine.

Shit.

She froze as her phone bounced off her lap and onto the floor.

The pressure from the gun went away, then a moment later the muzzle was pressed to her neck again, this time just behind her left ear.

Damn it. Why hadn't she checked the back seat?

"Keep those hands up. I'm going to relieve you of this." The pistol at her hip was pulled loose from its holster.

Great. Now he had two guns. Stella glanced into the rear view mirror. The figure in the back seat was mostly still in shadow but she could make out hard eyes behind the lenses of his glasses.

"You don't know what kind of trouble you're getting into," Stella said. "But if you're after money or the car, you can take it."

"Don't play dumb with me. You know what I'm here for. You're going to drive and we're going to have a little talk. Lock that door."

Stella moved her hand slowly toward the door. She glanced at Danny's condo building. There was no sign of him or anyone else out. If she wanted to survive this, getting out now might be her only chance.

The pressure from the gun increased, forcing her to cock her head.

"Don't even think about it. There's nowhere you can run from me."

That's when she caught a glint of silver in her peripheral vision. The way the man's wrist was cocked to get around the car's headrest made his watch visible. But not just any watch.

Shit.

It was Elton Stenger.

Her finger found the door lock button and pressed it.

"Now you drive."

Stella willed her body to comply. "Where am I going?" She started the car and shifted into drive.

"You're going to take me to the scientist."

Stella balked. Scientist? What was he talking about?

"I don't know any scientists."

The voice from the back seat changed to a growl. "I said don't play dumb with me, bitch." He punctuated the statement with a thrust from the gun, pressing her head forward.

"I'm sorry, I'm sorry!" Stella exclaimed. "I just need you to clarify for me. I meant . . . *which* scientist?"

"Quickly," the man snarled. "Your buddy accomplice in all this."

Stella's mind was reeling. Dr. Harold Quickly? The disappeared scientist from St. Petersburg? She'd never even met him. How was she supposed to find him in Los Angeles?

This was getting complicated. Swearing softly to herself, she eased the car out of the parking space and drove toward the exit. She glanced down and noted the still glowing screen of her Nokia in the footwell near her feet. Could she somehow call for help?

She needed to stall for time.

"How did you find me?" she asked. A passing street light briefly illuminated the back seat and she cast another glance in the mirror. Stenger's eyes were on the road. It had been over a decade since she had seen his body on the freeway. He had aged poorly. His already thin hair was gray at the temples and liver spots dotted his skin. He had a gaunt, cheerless face, and she noted a missing bottom tooth. Even so, he was undeniably more alive than the last time she saw him.

"Been waiting a long time for a break like this. Things are finally starting to go my way."

Stella tried to get her bearings. She knew practically nothing about navigating Los Angeles. She spotted a sign for Highway 101 and headed that way. Where was she going to take him?

She wiggled her left foot out of her shoe, slipping her heel free while keeping her eyes on the road.

"I think you might have the wrong idea about me," she said. "I'm barely involved in this case."

"The hell you aren't," Stenger spat. "Special Agent Stella York of the eff-bee-eye." He carefully enunciated each letter. "And I'm sure you got all your fed friends hanging around too. Bet you thought I'd be stupid and waltz right into your little trap. Don't think I didn't know what you were up to."

Damn.

Stella tried to think. It was clear he had the upper hand in every way here. She had to keep him talking.

"What tipped you off?"

"You think you could bait me close enough where someone could nab me? I saw who showed up. You didn't think I'd recognize the guy who ruined my life?"

Stella tried to process what he was saying. He was talking as if the rendezvous had already happened. What on earth was going on?

"Where's this scientist holed up now?" Stenger asked. "Where's he keeping all his time stuff?"

Stella fished around the footwell with her stockinged foot and tried to locate the phone with her toes. It seemed to have vanished.

"What kind of time stuff? There's a lot."

"I want the charger for this watch. The damn thing's blinking red on me already. You're gonna take me to where all the extra tech is. I want you to charge this thing up and fix it so my shit comes with me when I jump."

"Okay, I'll take you wherever you want," she said, turning the car onto the 101 on-ramp headed north. Where on earth would she go? The only equipment she knew of was at Carson's mansion. Her heel finally bumped something that felt like her phone. She slowly eased it forward till she could glance down and see the screen. She had to be sure Stenger wouldn't see what she was up to. Maybe if she had something to block his view? As she merged onto the 101, she glanced in the mirror again.

"I need to check my map, okay? It's in the glove box."

"Hell no."

"I don't know where I'm going without it."

"Stupid women drivers," Stenger muttered. "Can't get anywhere using their heads."

Stella grit her teeth and resisted the urge to throw an elbow at his face.

Stenger pulled the hammer back on her service pistol and pressed it to the right side of her head. "Okay, I got two guns on you now so you even think of pulling something fancy from that box and I'll let all the air out of your vacant head."

"You shoot me and we both die in a flaming car wreck," Stella countered. "Not that you aren't used to that."

Stenger stiffened. "What's that supposed to mean?"

Stella made a gut decision to run with it.

"I've already seen how you die. Didn't you know?"

"What are you talking about?"

"The other time travelers. They kick your ass all over the freeway." She stretched for the glove box.

Stenger jammed the gun into her ribs, making her wince. "The only one getting hurt today will be you if you don't watch your mouth."

Stella held up a hand, signaling that she understood, then

slowly opened the glove box. The map was resting atop a box of extra rounds for her Glock 23. She could feel Stenger's eyes on her as she removed the map and carefully shut the glove box.

"Give me that." Stenger snatched the map from her hand before she could open it. "You keep your eyes on the damn road."

Stella cursed under her breath.

But perhaps if he was caught up looking at the map, he wouldn't notice what she was up to in the front seat. She glanced at the screen of her phone in the footwell, pressing the volume control with her toe and turning it all the way down. Next she pressed the button for her recent calls. 911 would have been quicker, but with no way to talk to the dispatcher, she wasn't sure how she would communicate how to find her. Her phone number was linked to her address in Las Vegas so they wouldn't even know where to start. But Detective Danny Brigg's number was near the top of the recent calls screen. She held her breath and pressed the talk button with her big toe..

"Okay, I'm going to take you to where the time travel stuff is," Stella shouted to the back seat, raising her voice to cover any sound of the phone ringing on the open line. She glanced down to see if the phone was still ringing.

Come on, Danny. Pick up.

A distant click emanated from the phone.

"It's a mansion in West Hollywood!" She shouted again to drown out the "hello" from the other end.

"I'm not deaf, you dumb slut."

"I want to make sure you know I'm cooperating, Mr. Stenger," Stella enunciated. "And I'm going to take you there now. Three sixty-three Copa de Oro Drive. Can you find it on the map for me?"

"Wait. Copa de Oro? The dead musician's house? What are you trying to pull?"

"You said you wanted to go where all the time travel stuff is. It's at Carson Bradley's place. You said you wanted it, right?"

Stenger seemed at a loss for words so Stella merged left to catch the exit for Santa Monica Boulevard. As soon as she had made the offramp, she glanced down at her phone again. The screen read "Call Failed."

Shit. How much of the conversation had Danny been able to hear before the call dropped? Would it be enough?"

She tried to get her foot back on the phone to call again.

"Watch the damn road!" Stenger jabbed her with the end of the gun. She looked up just in time to swerve out of the lane and avoid a car braking ahead.

"Sorry!" Stella shouted.

"You trying to attract attention to us?" Stenger snarled.

"No! Just got distracted."

"Then keep your eyes out the damn window. I have to tell you again and I'll start shooting and to hell with the consequences."

Stella kept her eyes forward, but fished around again with her foot. The swerving from lane to lane seemed to have displaced the phone. Had it slid under the seat?

She cursed again and tried to come up with another plan. She tried to stare down other drivers, perhaps mouth a plea for help, but no other drivers met her eye. She considered swerving into a pole or causing an accident that could give her a chance to bolt, but the idea of setting an enraged killer loose on innocent civilians made her think twice. If he started shooting in the street, someone was bound to get hurt. She couldn't risk that, but she needed to find a way to bring him down now before she lost the chance forever.

They reached the affluent Bel Air neighborhood and were soon surrounded by high walls and privacy hedges that blocked any view of the homes from the road. In any other circumstances, the drive would have been beautiful. Elegantly styled topiaries and neatly manicured hedges were on display, but in the darkness they bore ominous, uncaring witness to her abduction.

Stella had hoped to see squad cars lining the street when they reached Carson's mansion, but the entrance was deserted. She pulled up to the code box that, like the walls, was overgrown with vines.

"I don't know the code." Stella said.

"Get out of the car."

Stella pulled forward a few feet, then put the car in park. Stenger climbed out of the back at the same time she exited the front. She walked around the front of the car with her hands up and stood between it and the closed gate. If they lingered here long enough, perhaps local PD would show up and end this.

"What now?"

"Shut up. I'm trying to think."

Stella finally had a good look at him. Stenger was shorter than she had imagined, He had a sort of stunted, wiry frame, but with a lean, muscled quality that reminded her of a wild animal that had survived too long on meager pickings.

"Turn around. Get up against that gate. Don't move."

Stenger backed away and set one of the guns down near the call box. Then he strode forward again and started tugging at his belt. He unbuttoned his pants and began kicking off his shoes as well.

What the hell?

Passing the pistol from one hand to the other, he pulled off his shirt and stripped out of the rest of his clothes as well.

"I don't know what you think is going to happen here, but there's no way that I'm going to let you—"

"Shut up!" Stenger shouted. "I said don't move."

The now naked man kicked his clothes into a pile near the front of the car, placing his glasses atop the pile last, then moved to the gate and crouched low, adjusting dials on his watch—his only remaining article of clothing. When he was finished messing with the device, he slowly lowered the gun. "You're going to be tempted to run. Tempted to go for this gun. I promise you won't have time." He set the gun on the ground at his feet, touched his watch hand to the gate, then grabbed it with his other hand and pressed something on the side. A moment later, he disappeared.

Stella blinked at the empty space next to the pistol.

Elton Stenger was gone.

She lunged for the gun.

"No! What did I just tell you!"

Stella froze, then slowly turned. The still naked Stenger was now standing next to the call box, pointing the second gun at her head.

The gate slid open.

"You lying to me?" Stenger snarled. "Because I walked through that house for the last ten minutes and didn't see anything you're talking about."

Stella felt like her brain was broken. It took a moment to even process what he was saying.

"It's . . . hidden," she stammered. "A secret room. I can show you."

Stenger picked up his discarded clothing and the second gun. He forced her to move the car through the now open gate onto Carson Bradley's property. They exited the vehicle again when they reached the fountain.

Stella was doing her best not to look at the naked man accompanying her, but the reality of what had just happened made her keep looking behind her, partly to be certain he was still there. Thankfully he at least pulled on pants. He put on his shirt as well but left it unbuttoned, stuffing his gun into the waistband of his pants, while keeping the Glock aimed at her.

He muttered as he checked his watch. She caught a glimpse of the glowing red light he had talked about.

Whatever hour or minute her captor had vanished to, it had clearly given him enough time to scale the wall, gain access to the house, open the gate and garage door, then jump back to the time he had left, arriving at the call box in time to pick up the gun and keep her from going anywhere. The logistics of the procedure he must have followed made her brain hurt, but she couldn't think of any other explanation.

What she was having the most trouble processing was the physical reality of seeing him vanish. She hadn't witnessed the moment he reappeared but she was sure it would have been just as disorienting. There had been no theatrics, no noise, only the slightest movement of the air around her, possibly rushing to fill the vacuum he had left behind.

Time travel.

Stenger gestured for her to lead the way through the garage. "You get any stupid ideas in here and I'll perforate you faster than you can blink."

Stella *wished* she had an idea. Even a stupid one, because she was running out of time.

If the police weren't here by now, that meant Danny likely hadn't heard much or any of her attempted SOS call. He was no doubt on the hunt for her, but depending on how much he had heard, he might be hours from figuring out where she was. She certainly didn't have that long. Once Stenger had what he wanted, she was dead.

She needed to stay useful, or at least keep him distracted.

"What you did back there at the gate . . . How did you learn that?"

"I've seen it done before," Stenger replied. "It's how they got away from me the first time."

Who was he talking about? Other time travelers?

She slowly made her way through the house toward the library where she knew the secret room was located.

"Why did you come back?" Stella asked. "You were in the

clear after St. Petersburg. The FBI couldn't find you. Nobody could. Why risk coming after Carson?"

"You think I was going to let him change things and do nothing about it? You know this shit was all built on lies, don't you?" He gestured to a rack of custom guitars mounted on the wall. "The songs and the movies. None of it was his. He took it from the other time! How much else was he going to change? He was screwing everything up. You have any idea how that was messing with me? What's the point knowing the future if you aren't even sure it's going to happen? The world ought to thank me for getting rid of him."

"You were worried he was changing the future?"

"He did change the future! I don't know how he did it. But things are all different now. Movies, music. That changed so it's changing everyone else, screwing with time. It's that 'squash a butterfly' business. Only he was stomping butterflies right and left, making a hundred other things different with every move."

Stella had read of the Butterfly Effect in her research, but hadn't stopped to consider that it was happening every day of Carson's life.

"Then how do you explain what *you're* doing? You must have changed things too."

"And I plan to change a lot more, believe me. But this time things are going to go *my* way."

Stella shook her head. All his posturing about Carson damaging the timeline was just sour grapes because he hadn't been able to do it himself.

They reached the library and Stella paused near the broad wooden desk.

"What will you do? Once you have his equipment?"

"Whatever the hell I want. Starting with getting even with the scientist."

The scientist again.

Stella had stalled as long as she could, but there was no more time. The door to Carson's vault lay just beyond the bookshelf. Once she opened it, there would be little chance of her surviving, and it would mean Stenger getting everything he wanted. A killer would not only remain on-the-loose, but now free to roam anywhere in time as well.

She couldn't let that happen.

Her heart was pounding, her instincts telling her she needed to run, to scream, to do anything to get out of here.

But after all of her work, she couldn't let him jump away and never come back.

Or could she?

An idea struck her.

He'd been forced to put the gun down in order to jump. It wouldn't go with him. And if the watch was as low on power as he seemed to think, maybe him jumping away would be the exact thing she needed him to do. It would buy her the time she desperately needed.

With Stenger blocking the exit from the library, she was defenseless. She didn't even have any weapons at her disposal.

Well, maybe there was one.

She took a deep breath and adopted what she hoped was an awed tone. "Can I say one thing?"

Stenger narrowed his eyes, clearly suspicious.

It made her nauseated to even be trying this, but she was an FBI agent, damn it. There was no way she was letting him win.

If she could just get close to the watch . . .

"It's just, you must be so *smart* to have figured this stuff out all by yourself. I have to admit, it's kind of . . . sexy."

She held his gaze. She thought there was no way he was going to fall for it, but she waited breathlessly, biting her lip.

"Well, it wasn't easy. I can tell you that," Stenger muttered.

Maybe she had a chance.

"I think it's incredible," she said brushing her hair back behind her ear. She then let her fingers trail down the neckline of her shirt, her fingertips brushing the exposed skin at the tops of her breasts. "I mean, we've been hunting for you forever and you always elude capture. But I have to admit, part of the reason I was so excited to be on this case was that I wanted to meet you. You're our number one most wanted. Everyone in the Bureau knows your name."

Elton Stenger's mouth twitched. It was the briefest hint of a smile. "It's about time I get some recognition. They don't know the half of what I done."

"Can I—can I look at it?" She pointed the watch. "It's so beautiful."

Stenger tilted the face of the chronometer toward her. Her fingers drifted toward it as she studied the various rings and fobs. Which one had he pressed to activate it? Jessica had said it was a pin on the side . . .

"Hey, no touching." Stenger recoiled.

"Sorry, it's just so cool."

"Let's see this secret room already." Stenger waved the gun. "I don't have time for distractions."

The spell was broken.

Stella winced and turned toward the mantlepiece. She reached for the award trophy she had seen Jessica use and gave it a twist. The bookcase to the right of the fireplace slid open, revealing the secret doorway.

"Well, I'll be damned," Stenger muttered. "You were telling the truth."

He took a step forward, then hesitated, his eyes on Stella. "Don't be thinking you can shut me in there."

He snatched up a log from the basket of firewood and positioned it in the track of the sliding bookcase, then he grabbed her by the arm and hauled her into the doorway ahead of him, the gun pressed to her lower back.

"Any booby traps?"

"Not that I know of," Stella said.

"Let's see you find out for sure." He shoved her forward.

Stella stumbled a few feet and regained her balance as she reached the microwave-sized gravitizer. She turned and gestured toward it. "This is what you are looking for, right? So your clothes can stay on?"

"Find me the charger."

Stella had no idea what the charger for a time travel device even looked like, but imagined it had to have some manner of adapter plug on one end to work in any of the electrical sockets. She scoured the room for outlets, noting the sliding bookcase had closed again, bumping into the log Stenger had laid in the track. Only a narrow gap remained as an exit.

She kept an eye on Stenger as she searched. Once he had what he wanted, how much longer would she be alive? She tried to breathe and calm her nerves.

Stenger took the opportunity to shove his clothes into the gravitizer box, stripping back out of his pants and shirt. He fiddled with the controls to try to activate it. After punching a few buttons and flipping a lever, the gravitizer began to glow with an eerie blue light.

Stella scanned the cubby holes lining the walls and noted that one held a portable fire extinguisher bottle. She eased herself closer.

That's when she spotted the basket with a charger cord resting near Carson's open logbook.

While Stenger was preoccupied with getting on his newly gravitized pants, Stella bundled the charger cord into her left hand and backed up against the cubby with the fire extinguisher. With her right hand behind her back, she felt for the handle of the extinguisher.

"Is this what you're looking for?" she asked, extending her open palm with the charger cord.

"About time," Stenger said, reaching for it. Stella brought her palm back a few inches, causing Stenger to take a step toward her.

She brought the fire extinguisher around and swung it as hard as she could at his head. Stenger ducked forward and the extinguisher missed his skull, striking him at the juncture of his upper back and the base of his neck instead. He groaned and staggered forward into the countertop.

Stella dropped the extinguisher and bolted for the door, kicking the fireplace log loose and leaping through the narrow gap in one motion. She spun around to shove the bookcase door closed. She heard it click just before the gunshots erupted from inside the room. Two books were blasted from the shelf beside her, bits of paper scattering in the air as the bullets passed through. A third book struck her knee and a searing hot pain lanced though her lower thigh.

Stella dove behind the desk and rolled, getting back to her feet a moment later and scrambling toward the door. Her heart was racing, but not as fast as the rest of her. She crashed into the library door, flinging it the rest of the way open and sprinting for the front of the house. She could see the expansive living area at the end of the hallway but the moment she stepped into it, she was caught in the face by a swinging fist.

She went down hard, spinning and slamming into the floor face first.

Her ears rang and her vision swam with tiny stars. Her eye socket felt like she had been struck with a mallet.

When she rolled over and opened her eyes, Stenger was looming over, still half naked. His foot came down on her gut in a merciless kick, causing her to gasp and curl into a ball on the floor. She writhed in pain.

Stella gasped and coughed.

He was so fast. Too fast.

The floor was slick with blood and she realized it was coming from her leg. In the rush from the room, she had barely noticed the wound, but now it was on fire.

"You think you could pull one over on me!" Stenger screamed.

Stella rolled to her knees and tried to scramble away, but he was on top of her in a flash, grabbing her by the hair and yanking her head back. She shrieked as he pulled her upright. He clawed at her hand, then yanked the charger cord from her fist. He proceeded to wrap it around her neck, choking her airway.

"No!" Stella realized too late what he was doing and clawed at the cord with her nails but he had already pulled it tight against her skin. She yanked on the arm he had around her neck but he was too strong. She tried to throw an elbow back into his ribs but he simply absorbed the blow.

"You can never escape me!" Stenger hissed.

Stella managed to get her feet under her and with a desperate push, stood and thrust Stenger backward. They crashed into the wall next to the living room fireplace, then reeled across the room, glancing off chairs before colliding with a low railing that divided the living room's theater area from a separate sitting room. Stella attempted to force Stenger backward over the railing, but her leg gave out.

Stella fell to her knees and Stenger went down on top of her, his right hand still pulling on the cord around her neck, his left palm braced against the floor near her face.

She struggled for breath, her fingers scrabbling uselessly against the tension of the charging cord. Stenger's hot breath was in her ear as he struggled to restrain her. She railed against his grip on her, but her energy was fading. The last burst of adrenaline had only gotten her so far and she no longer had the strength to fight. Her lungs burned.

Oh God.

This was how she was going to die. Murdered by a time traveling serial killer no one even believed existed.

Why had she ever tried to find him?

Her chest spasmed. Blackness was closing in. She tried desperately to pull on the cord around her neck with one hand while her other struggled to hold her weight up. But she lacked even the strength to do that anymore. Her vision narrowed until all that she could see was Stenger's hand planted on the floor next to her.

But not just his hand.

The watch.

The blackness was beckoning. Her vision faded to a single point, but she used the last moments of her consciousness to focus on the watch. She took the hand from her neck and she could only claw at the watch feebly with it, but her fingertips found the bezel and the fobs on the side and one catch that toggled sideways to access a pin. The circular rings of the watch shimmered in her fading vision. It was a thing of beauty. Silver and black and a pretty little arrow pointing to a setting for one minute.

As the blackness closed around her completely, she stretched her hand for the watch, fumbled with the safety, and pressed the pin.

STELLA HIT the floor with her face again, this time the pain made her gasp.

Air.

Good God there was air.

She gulped at it with her mouth wide, swallowing it down so

fast she coughed and retched. She gasped again and rolled over. Her bloody leg lit up with fire again and she gasped once more in pain, but even that was a relief because she had air.

She clawed at her neck, a frantic movement, but her fingertips found only the impressions on her skin. No charger cord. It had vanished.

Stenger had vanished.

The realization finally registered.

It had worked! He was gone.

But for how long?

The haze of her mind cleared.

A minute. The watch had read a minute.

He was coming back.

How long had she been writhing on the floor? Ten seconds? Fifteen?

She forced herself to her feet, wincing again from the pain in her leg. How far could she get in forty-five seconds? She started to stumble for the door.

But then she stopped.

No.

She wasn't going to run. Not this time.

Her pulse was pounding, keeping a beat inside her skull like a metronome.

No. Like a clock.

Thirty seconds?

She turned back, scanning the living room until her eyes found the set of fireplace tools near the big stone hearth. She hurled herself toward it, the clock in her head ticking relentlessly. She was weak. Her leg was slick with blood and dragged behind her as she limped, but she wouldn't go down. Not now. Not yet.

Covering the distance across the living room took an eternity. Her hurt foot caught on the rug and she stumbled, falling to her knees.

But her hand closed around the handle of the fire tongs.

The feel of the cold iron gave her strength.

But when she turned around again, she knew it was a lost cause. The distance back across the room seemed to expand into miles. She was never going to get back in the seconds she had remaining. Ten? Nine? Her chest was heaving, her head pounding.

Seconds till he was back. Then death would be swift.

Three seconds. Two. She wouldn't wait any longer. Stella took a deep breath and screamed her rage as she hurled the fire tongs. They soared across the room and time seemed to slow.

And all she had done was send a futile projectile into empty space.

In her weakness, the fire tongs hadn't even reached all the way to where she was aiming. They clattered to the floor uselessly.

The clock in her head was screaming an alarm.

Time was up.

Her fingers wrapped around the handle of the fire poker and she used all of her remaining strength to hurl it.

Stella watched with bated breath. But like the tongs, the poker failed to reach the spot she had aimed for. Her heart sank, but then the tip of the poker hit the floor and it bounced, arcing onward again—directly into the sudden apparition of Elton Stenger who, at that instant, reappeared on the floor.

The half-naked man let out a shriek and went over sideways, not so much struck by the iron poker as impaled by it. He was flung to his side and then over again onto his front, and laid still.

17 / TIME CRIME

Special Agent Stella York stared at the man on the floor in a daze. He wasn't bloody but he was completely still. The end of the fire poker protruded from his torso like an extra appendage more than a weapon. It was as though the poker and the man were now one and the same.

She refused to take her eyes off him until the sound of sirens slowly penetrated the fog around her mind.

As the air filled with sound, she crawled slowly across the floor, found the dead man's wrist, unfastened the chronometer the way Jessica had instructed, and yanked it free. She then squirmed back across the floor to rest her back against one of the armchairs, clenching the device tightly in both hands.

A uniformed police officer was the first one to find her, his gun drawn and expression hard. He was immediately joined by a half dozen more. They asked questions, searched the other rooms, but Stella was slow to respond. She extracted her FBI badge from her pocket and flashed it at them. That seemed to change the mood. But it was only when a pair of crystalline blue eyes met hers that any words finally registered.

"I've got you. I'm getting you out of here."

Detective Danny Briggs scooped her up and carried her out

the front of Carson's mansion. An ambulance pulled through the now open gate. The circular drive was packed with vehicles. Red and blue lights flashed and reflected from every one of the mansion's multitude of windows.

Stella winced as she was laid on a stretcher, but Danny stayed by her side.

"You are one crazy woman, you know that? I said 'promise me you won't try to take this guy on by yourself,' and what do you do?"

"Wasn't exactly my idea," Stella muttered as she laid back.

"I'm glad you're okay."

The paramedics pushed in to attend to her and she did her best to answer their questions. Yes, she was shot. No, just in the leg. They poked and prodded and inspected her. There was an exit wound and the bullet hadn't hit any major blood vessels but they wanted a doctor to have a good look at it. She was bandaged and told to stay still.

She stuffed the chronometer in her pocket.

When they were satisfied at her condition, Detective Briggs was allowed into the back of the ambulance to sit with her.

"So, you finally got him," he said, picking up her hand and pressing it between his. "How does it feel?"

Stella squeezed his hand back and allowed herself a smile. "It's about time."

IF SHE COULD HAVE HAD her way, she would have done without the hospital stay, but the one advantage to the overnight visit was that it gave her an excuse to delay her conversation with SAC Devers from the bureau office in Las Vegas. As she checked herself out of the hospital, she knew she couldn't put it off any longer. When he picked up, it was clear from his tone that her excursion hadn't gone over well.

"Do you mind explaining to me how one of my agents ends up involved in a murder investigation in California working a case she hasn't been assigned to in thirteen years?"

The rest of the conversation went about as well.

By the end of the call, Stella was facing a fourteen day suspension and a possible meeting with the Office of Professional Responsibility.

When she hung up with her boss, Stella simply stood there. She pulled the purloined time travel watch from her pocket and stared at it. Over a decade of searching. Was this all she had to show for it?

She was startled from her daze by the phone ringing again. It was a number she didn't recognize. She picked it up reflexively.

"Hello?"

"Good morning, Miss York, do you have a moment to talk about the advertisement you posted in the newspaper?"

Stella sighed. "I'm sorry to waste your time. That wasn't a real posting. It was part of a criminal investigation. It's over now."

"I don't believe it's over just yet. You do still have the chronometer, don't you?"

Stella frowned and looked down at the device in her hand. "I'm sorry, who are you?"

"My name is Doctor Harry Quickly and I'd very much like to meet with you."

Harold Quickly?

The scientist.

"Um. Yes. I actually have so many questions for you." Stella felt around her pockets for a notepad.

"Let's meet at the location you suggested in the ad. Exposition Park? Near the rose garden. You said noon."

Stella glanced at her watch. "Wait, that doesn't give me a lot of time to—"

"I'll see you there." The call ended and Stella found herself staring at her phone's home screen.

She limped her way out of the hospital lobby to the cab stand.

Stella checked her watch again as she slid into the cab. "Exposition Park. As fast as you can get me there."

THE EXPOSITION PARK Rose Garden sprawled over seven acres. The tall bushes would have provided excellent concealment for law enforcement agents, had Stella really been setting up her sting operation. But with Elton Stenger dead, the view was a lot more relaxing. The midday sun shone brightly on the myriad varieties of roses in bloom and the sky held not a single cloud. To her satisfaction, Stella had arrived with over five minutes to spare. She overtipped the cabbie and then wandered slowly along the grassy lanes of the garden, nursing her aching leg and keeping an eye out for someone who looked like they were looking for her.

She was wearing her badge and sidearm openly on her hip, which drew occasional glances from passersby, but otherwise she moved unmolested.

Several tourists with cameras were snapping photos of the roses and she even spotted a few artists set up with easels. She wandered into the center of the garden, trailing a mother and daughter both sporting sweatshirts with the Trojan emblem of the neighboring University of Southern California. The pair were chatting amiably about the girl's college life, but when they turned right down a neighboring lane, Stella froze.

Ahead in the grass aisle, not more than fifty yards from her, stood Elton Stenger.

He was staring down a perpendicular avenue, his expression intent on his search.

"What the hell?" Stella swore and reached for her gun.

She had nearly cleared it from her holster when a strong hand closed over her wrist. She spun to find an old man in a tweed vest standing behind her. She jolted and wrenched her wrist free of his grasp.

"Don't." The old man said calmly. "Wait."

Stella aimed her pistol at him and backed away a step. "Who the hell are—"

"One more moment," the old man said. He held up a finger, his gaze somewhere behind her. Stella spun around again and located Stenger. He was staring straight back at her. But then he lunged to one side, racing away down the path and sprinting out of the garden.

Stella moved to follow but the old man called to her again.

"You can relax! It's done now."

Stella turned to guard herself against the old man again, watching him warily. But nothing about his posture suggested a threat. He had a kindly face, well-tanned with good humored crinkles at the corners of his eyes. He smiled.

"I've been waiting a long time to meet you, Miss York. I'm Harry."

Stella's heart was still racing from having sighted Stenger. She glanced again toward the exit of the rose garden. "That man —is supposed to be dead!"

"And he is," Harry replied, keeping an outstretched palm toward her. "He just doesn't know it yet. Come on. Let's walk. I have a feeling we have a lot to talk about."

Stella slowly lowered her gun.

The old man gestured for her to follow him, and they walked back the way she had come, away from the exit Stenger had disappeared through.

In a patient and pleasant tone, the old scientist began to talk.

"We had to close the loop, you see? The events that happened to you yesterday began today. Elton Stenger, having seen us together here in the park, will now jump back in time to find you. He'll ascertain who you are, follow you, and take you captive from the back of your own vehicle. The rest of yesterday's events will unfold as they did. You've already lived through them, but they are an end that Mr. Stenger has yet to experience."

Stella recalled Stenger's rant in the car the night before about having seen her with Harry Quickly. It made sense now.

"What about where he came from? Two-thousand and nine. Whatever brought him here. Will all that still happen?"

As they walked, Harry told her the tale of the five friends from 2009 and their accidental displacement through time due to a lab accident at the Temporal Studies Society. He explained his connection to Malcolm and how, if it hadn't been for the actions of this misfit band of time travelers she had encountered, he would have ended up as one of Stenger's victims.

Carson Bradley was dead, but in another timeline, his friends had come back to save him. She had witnessed Stenger's end on the Interstate at the diversion of that timeline. Somewhere, in some time, the whole lot of them were now safe and alive.

"I don't think you'll have any negative effects from having experienced that particular paradox," the scientist said. "But I hope you'll stay in touch if you do. This is all very much a new field of study for all of us. But as far as Elton Stenger is concerned, that danger is over."

"A closed loop," Stella muttered. "So what does that mean for the future?"

"An excellent question. I think that depends largely on you. How do you feel about your future? Any changes you'd like to make?"

By now they had wandered across Exposition Boulevard via the pedestrian walkway and on through the USC campus. She noticed that she had been so wrapped up in the scientist's explanation that her leg hadn't bothered her at all. She found herself staring up at a beautiful red and gold clock with four faces on it that sat at the edge of Alumni Park.

"You make it sound like I have some choice in all this," Stella said. "But I'm not like you." She reached into her pocket and removed the beautiful silver chronometer. She held it out to him. "I think this might be what you're after. It won't do me any good."

Harry Quickly took the device and played with a few of the dials, then slipped it into his pocket. "I'm going to tell you something I probably shouldn't. But if you promise not to report me to the time travel authorities, I can give you some insight into the future."

"I don't know any time travel authorities."

"Not yet," Harry said.

Stella narrowed her eyes. "You know what's going to happen to me?"

"I know a few things that are pretty certain. For one, this case of yours—the deaths in Saint Pete and the murder of Carson Bradley—won't be reopened. A young Elton Stenger in Florida will go to jail for the killings. Your reports on the subject will mysteriously vanish, and the anomaly of the existence of two Elton Stengers is going to be swept under the rug. In a matter of weeks, all evidence of the existence of time travel will be erased from this timeline. The general public will never be the wiser."

"They're going to cover this up? The truth about the existence of time travel has to be the most world-changing information that the human race has ever discovered."

"Which is precisely why the powers that be don't want it out. Not yet anyway. It's almost the new millennium of course. The time is coming."

"Why cover up my work then? I've sacrificed my career getting to the bottom of this." Stella felt the heat rising in her cheeks. "I've been through *hell* for this. What gives them the right to take that away from me?"

"That's something I thought you might like to ask them yourself." The old man reached into an inside pocket of his vest and extracted a business card. It was gloss black with silver lettering. She took the card and read the organization name. "Time Crimes?"

"It's a division of the Allied Scientific Coalition of Time Travelers. As an organization, I don't often see eye-to-eye with them on their methods, but that number will put you through to a time when one of the contacts I trust is running the Temporal Crime Investigation Division. Her name is Doctor Noelle Chun. She was a professor before she took on this job."

"A woman is in charge of the organization? That's certainly a plus," Stella said.

"She won't be born for another hundred years, but leave a message. She'll get back to you. Word on the street is that she's looking for more agents she can trust. She told me to keep an eye out for anyone I thought might be a good candidate."

"Time crimes," Stella murmured, studying the card.

"You already caught one dangerous time traveler, and you're good at it. Thought you might want a shot at more."

Stella glanced up at the multi-faced clock again. She could leave Vegas. Possibly leave this whole timeline? Suddenly it seemed like the future was full of possibilities. "With all these diverging timelines, how do I know which future is the right choice for me?"

She turned back to the old man, but found she was staring at empty space.

Stella turned slowly in place, searching the grounds of the campus around her.

Harry Quickly had vanished.

Stella stood open-mouthed for several seconds, still scanning the grounds, then she shook her head.

No one was ever going to believe her.

Her Nokia vibrated in her pocket, and when she pulled it out, she noted that she had a new voicemail from Danny's number. She also noticed that the battery symbol was down to its last bar.

She suspected she only had enough power left for one call.

Stella bit her lip and glanced up at the clock again.

Then she dialed the number on the card.

The phone made a strange pulsing noise before going straight to the beep of a voicemail.

She took a deep breath.

"Hi. My name is Special Agent Stella York, and I'm ready to get to work."

THE CHRONOTHON SNEAK PEEK.

"Time travel is hard. Let's get that straight first thing. If you think any part of this will be simple, you can stop now and have a safe, happy, life. Of course, if you're reading this, you're likely not content with safe."-Journal of Dr. Harold Quickly, 2037

I feel very alive considering I haven't been born yet.

Across the expanse of grasses and water stretching to the distant shoreline, the rumbling of rocket engines is causing the wild birds to take to the air in droves. As they stream past my perch on top of the abandoned radio tower, their cries are lost in the roar of the machine beyond them. I have a clear view of the amber glow from the Saturn V rocket. Apollo 11 is hoisting humanity's dreams toward the heavens in a historic panorama in front of me, but I can't stop looking at the girl.

This is the third day I've woken up and existed as an affront to the laws of nature. I've bent them before of course, but this is the first time I've journeyed beyond my own lifetime—what should have been my lifetime in any case—and she's the one who got me into this.

Mym's arms are draped on the lower railing while her legs swing gently as they dangle over the edge. Her chin is propped on her arms and her blue eyes are on the rocket streaming its way skyward. After a moment they narrow slightly. "You know, Ben, I may stop taking you awesome places if you aren't even going to pay attention." Her voice is scolding, but when she turns her head, her eyes are playful. She tries to hold her mouth tight in an expression of aggravation, but as I glower back at her, her cheeks start creeping upward until she's grinning uncontrollably.

My legs are crossed below me, a safe distance back from the edge of the platform. A month ago, I wouldn't have dreamed of being this high up. A lot of things have changed about me in a month. For one, I used to stay in my own time. The chronometer on my wrist changed that. Mym's dad let me keep it. I did save his life, but I don't believe that was his reason for letting me have it. I think he wanted to let me into this world of his—the world where time is no longer about straight lines, but about paths not taken, a secret world where consecutive events in your life don't have to be consecutive at all.

Last night, we caught the Beatles in their last concert at Candlestick Park. This morning, I ate my breakfast a table away from Salvador Dali at a café in Spain, and still made it here to Florida in time for the launch. Not a moment was wasted in airport security or waiting for a calendar page to turn.

Mym leans back onto her hands and watches the twisting trail of rocket smoke dissipate in the wind. She looks happy.

"Do you just wake up amazed every day?" I ask.

She tilts her gaze toward me. "Don't you?"

"I do now. This is incredible. It's like every day is your birthday, or Christmas."

"I know a guy who does that." She smiles. "He only does birthdays and holidays. I think every day should be a good day though, if you're doing it right."

"Well, this certainly makes that a lot easier." I twist the dials on my chronometer. "You get to pick out the really good days."

Mym studies me briefly then turns skyward again. "It's easier to have good days now." She closes her eyes, soaking in the sunshine. I nod, though I know she can't see me. In the excitement of our traveling the past couple of days, I sometimes forget that she spent the last few years trying to find a way to keep her father from being murdered. It hasn't been all good days. But she doesn't seem to be thinking about that now. Her face is relaxed, her skin lit by the sun. She looks young. I wonder again how old she is. *Early twenties? Does she even know?* If I hadn't spent the last quarter century with my days encapsulated in sequential boxes, if Thursday could come after Sunday or spring follow fall, would I know my age? Would I feel it somehow? Would I care?

Mym is still an enigma to me. As I watch her chest slowly rising and falling with each breath, I wonder—not for the first time—why she picked me to come with her on this adventure. She's the type of girl who doesn't seem to realize the effect she has on people. I'm the opposite. I feel like I've always known where I stand. I get a few glances from the girls, maybe not all of them, but the ones who don't mind a guy who gets his hands dirty for a living–the ones who don't run off if I occasionally let a long swim at the beach pass for a shower, or pick them up for a date on my old motorcycle. I used to know where I stood anyway until I met her—a petite, blonde time traveler with a taste for adventure. Now it's like starting over.

I let my gaze drift back to the now vacant sky. "So where's the next stop?"

She opens her eyes. "Hmm. We're still in the sixties. Anything else you want to catch while you're here, or do you want to head to the seventies?"

"You're the pro at this. I'm totally at your mercy."

"Ooh. Totally?"

"Um, maybe I'm going to regret that."

"Nope. You said totally. I know exactly where I'm taking

you." She swings her legs up, tucking one underneath her, and faces me.

"Oh God. That smirk on your face is scaring me. Where are we going?"

"You just dial the settings." She rifles through her messenger bag and hands me a long silver tube and a hard rubber wheel. It takes me a moment to identify the wheel without the rest of its parts, but then it dawns on me.

"We're going roller skating?"

"Better. It's roller disco!" She beams. "Degravitize that."

"Oh Lord. Disco?" I roll my eyes, but set to work with the silver degravitizer, scanning it across the roller skate wheel like Mym taught me, removing the gravitite particles inside that enabled it to follow us through time. I consider objecting to the idea, but I have to be honest with myself, I'd probably follow her anywhere.

"So where does one go to roller disco in the seventies?"

"The beginning." Mym rummages around and removes more items.

"And where is the beginning?"

"Brooklyn." She's intent on something in her hands. "I'm taking you to The Empire."

She's studying a photo of a shelf with an iron, a bowl of whisks, and a pair of purple suede roller skates on it.

"Is that at the roller rink?"

"No. We can't make it to The Empire straight from here. It's too far to jump with these chronometers. That's okay, we need to stop and pick up my skates anyway." She stands and adjusts her satchel, then sticks her hand out for the wheel. I toss it to her, and she sets it precariously on the railing. "Okay. Don't shake the tower."

I step cautiously toward her. "What's the date?"

"May 18th, 1973. 1600 Zulu."

I dial the time into my chronometer and reach for the top of the roller skate wheel. "We good on elevation?"

Mym extends a tape measure to the platform at our feet and checks the height of the railing. "Perfect."

My right hand is poised atop my chronometer, the fingertips of my chronometer hand pressed to the wheel, keeping firm contact to our anchor in real time.

"Wait. Hang on." Mym squints at the photo and then rotates the wheel 180 degrees. "We don't want to end up in the floor." She grins up at me. "Ready?"

"Ready as I'm going to be." I eye the long drop from the platform, then quickly bring my attention back to the wheel. Once we're gone, the wheel will likely tumble to the ground, but we'll be years away.

"Three . . . two . . . one . . . push."

I press the pin on the side of my chronometer and blink.

The room smells like dust and potpourri. I take my fingers off the roller skate on the shelf in front of me and eye my surroundings. Old women are picking through clothing racks and bric-a-brac as dim light filters through dingy subterranean windows. In the corner, the cash register drawer dings as it shuts. The chime blends with the muffled sounds of car horns and traffic.

"You keep your skates in a thrift store?"

"It's not easy to find purple suede skates in my size." Mym picks up the skates and holds them to her cheek. "And they have rainbow laces. You have to snatch treasure up when you find it."

"I guess so." I smile and follow her toward the counter. I almost collide with her as she stops at a rack of sunglasses and plucks a pair of men's aviators from among them. She turns and slips them on.

"What do you think?"

"Um, I think they're a little big for your face."

She considers me briefly. "I feel bad for you."

"What? Why?"

"Because you're going to have to keep looking at them. I love them." She grins and spins back toward the counter. A bell rings as the door to the basement shop opens and a gust of wind follows a middle-aged woman inside. It brings the smell of truck exhaust and hot dogs. I step toward the door and grab it before it closes. Outside, the concrete steps lead upward to a sidewalk full of foot traffic, and beyond the road, a six-story apartment building. I glance back briefly at Mym paying for her skates and then climb upward into the urban noise.

Cabs and trucks clog the street as pedestrians stream past me, a fashionable mix of wide collars and ties, plaid bellbottoms, paisley shirts, and a smattering of turtlenecks and sweater vests. I stand on the top step of the thrift store entrance and breathe in 1973 New York. Despite the exhaust and a faint odor of trash, there is a tang of salt breeze in the air and a pleasant mix of ethnic foods. After a few moments, Mym joins me. "It's great, right?"

"Sure is busy."

"Well, it's the middle of the day in Manhattan."

"Where's this place we're going skating?"

"It's in Brooklyn, but that's not for a couple of years yet. Come on, you want to grab lunch?"

"Yeah, I could eat."

"There's this little Italian place called Angelina's on Mulberry Street that has the most amazing calzones. It's a bit of a walk, but it's worth it."

"I'm in."

It's cool in the shade of the buildings, and I relish the brief moments of sun on my bare arms as we traverse the corner crosswalk. I dodge pedestrians while trying to keep up with Mym's brisk pace as she plunges into the shadow of the next building. She moves with the confidence of someone at home in her surroundings, flitting among the foot traffic with fluid ease, her purple skates hung casually over one shoulder. I narrowly miss being run down by a bicycle and stuff my hands into my jeans pockets to make myself a little thinner. As I skirt past a pair of rabbis, I find Mym waiting for me near a streetlight.

"Come on, pokey. I want to beat the lunch rush."

"Hey, I take up a lot more space than you do. I think these people treat that as a sin."

"People here live fast." She observes me over the rim of her new sunglasses. "Better learn to keep up." She winks before leading the way on. I appreciate her figure as she walks away, watching the curves that my hands have yet to touch. I entertain the thought for just a moment, then jog to catch up.

"You come to New York a lot?" I fall into step beside her.

"I try to. There are some great people here."

"There's certainly enough to choose from."

Mym slows to look at me. "You've never been to New York?"

"I passed through once as a kid with my parents, but I've never explored it as an adult."

"Then today is your lucky day. After lunch I can give you the tour."

"You going to show me the constructing of the Empire State Building?"

"Hmm, that would be a long way back," she muses. "Although I've always wanted to get a picture of me like one of those guys eating lunch up on the girders over the city. We might have to add that to the extended tour."

"Ha. You'll have to have one of the workers snap that shot. No way you're getting me out there on one of those."

"You just wait, Ben. A few weeks of traveling with me, and we'll have those heights issues vanquished."

My heartbeat quickens. I haven't asked how long she plans on traveling around with me. The idea of getting weeks with her makes me feel happy enough that I imagine I might be coaxed onto a few girders after all. I try not to show the eagerness on my face. "I guess we'll see."

An opening shop door halts me in my tracks as a group of women spills out onto the sidewalk from a boutique. A pretty young mother snags a wheel of her stroller on the doorstop, bringing the ladies behind her to a halt. I grab the door handle and open the door farther to help her extricate it.

"Thanks so much." The woman smiles, and another half dozen ladies thank me as I hold the door for their exit. The press of women moves onward along the sidewalk and I stretch to peer over their heads.

Mym is three shops down, shaking her head, but smiling. As I close the door behind the last straggler, another figure lurches up from the next shop entrance. In a tattered corduroy coat and porous straw fedora, he ricochets off a planter near the doorway and staggers toward the women. The group parts like a flock of swallows, reconvening beyond him with titters of consternation and a few hands held to noses.

The vagrant ignores the slight and tips his fedora in delayed cordiality, but stays his stumbling course toward me. I step to the side, but he sways with me, reaching out to my arms, raised to avert our collision. His right hand wraps around my wrist and clamps it with a near painful strength.

"Whoa, buddy. You doing okay?" I plant my other hand against his chest, to keep him at a distance and prop him up. His lean face is lined and dirty, but his stark, gray eyes have a sharp clarity despite his unbalanced state. I recoil from the scent of stale beer and halitosis, but before I can free my wrist from his grasp, he teeters and falls, dragging my arm across my body and down to the ground. Pain shoots up my wrist as my palm strikes the concrete and my vision suddenly goes dark. I've landed partially atop the vagrant, my other hand outstretched to the sidewalk beyond his head. I jerk my left arm out of his grip and jolt back to my feet. The world is changed.

Shaded sunlight has been replaced with an ink black sky. Streetlights illuminate sidewalks only populated by a few restaurant patrons retreating into the night. Mym is gone. I spin around and search the way I've come. I've been displaced. I check my chronometer. It still reads the settings I had from my last jump. *How is that possible? Shouldn't I have ended up on this sidewalk in daylight?*

The vagrant is struggling to get back to his feet. His left hand is crushing his straw hat as he tries to get his legs under him. He stretches a hand out to me for assistance. I sigh and grab his wrist, pulling a little more firmly than necessary. On his feet, the man gives me a scowl. "You didn't have to knock me down!" This is followed by a jerk as he pulls his arm from my grip and staggers toward the wall, a trail of slurred curses in his wake.

I look back to my surroundings and rub my wrist. My pulse throbs against the band of my chronometer. I gingerly remove it and hold it in my hand. This is the second time I've injured my wrist in a week. It was only just beginning to heal from the first fall. On that occasion, I plummeted out a window trying to save my friend. I considered myself lucky to have walked away with just a sprain. Getting knocked down by a random homeless man seems far less worthwhile.

I recheck my chronometer settings. Still set to 1600 Zulu. *So how is it nighttime? Did the jolt from the fall break it?* I study the different concentric rings, seeing if anything is amiss. Nothing is wrong externally. I give it a shake and listen for anything loose inside. Nothing.

Shit. What am I supposed to do now? I look around, hoping that at any moment Mym will suddenly appear to scold me for being careless and take us along our way. There is no one except a cab driver sitting outside a bar at the end of the block, his hazard lights pulsing their warning to the night. At a loss for what to do, I walk back the way I've come. The streets are less inviting in the darkness. The towering buildings no longer look inspiring, but loom overhead on the fringe of night, lifeless hulks obliterating the stars.

I slip my chronometer onto my other wrist and fidget with the dials. I consider trying to jump back to the time I left. *Will it still work? I don't even know how far I've gone. Will I have enough power to get back?* My mind goes back to Dr. Quickly's lessons, and the varied tales he told of ways time travelers could meet their demise. They involved everything from fusing into walls to flinging yourself off the planet into the void of space. *Those were things that could happen with a working chronometer. What about if it's broken? Am I going to blink myself out of existence?* I've heard stories of time travelers not anchoring themselves properly for a jump and vanishing completely. Some say there is a place you go that exists outside of time, but there the line between science and urban legend starts to blur. Every time traveler learns early on to avoid that scenario.

Those lessons feel as though they're a long time ago, though for me it's only been a matter of weeks. History would say it hasn't happened yet. It will be nearly a decade till I'm even born, farther still when I'll first be sent through time. But this is time travel. Middles can come before beginnings, and it's anyone's guess where the end might be.

As I cross to the next block, I glance down the side street and note a cluster of young men loitering on the stoop of an apartment building. A dozen eyes follow my progress. Without my usual method of escape, I feel suddenly vulnerable under their gaze. I check myself to keep from walking faster. I continue with feigned ease for another half block until I'm well out of sight, and then stop.

Get yourself together, Ben. You're fine. You're just in New York... in 1973. I glance back at the vacant street behind me and then force myself to think. *What now?* I do a mental inventory of my belongings. Besides a possibly broken chronometer, my possessions are down to a wallet, pen, Swiss Army knife, and Mym's degravitizer that I forgot to put back in her backpack. I also have Dr. Quickly's worn leather journal stuck in my back pants pocket. I pull that out and walk a few steps toward the nearest streetlamp to read it. I flip through the handwritten scribbles and drawings, searching for the section on the workings of the chronometer. The book had been a gift, but a utilitarian one, filled with the carefully depicted details of a lifetime of research.

I stop on a page showing a partially disassembled chronometer. Staring at the drawing of the component parts, I immediately realize I'm out of my depth. *Even if I had the tools, there's no way I would even be able to recognize what was broken.* I slap the journal shut. A murmur alerts me that the men from the stoop have moved to the corner behind me. The tallest of the bunch is eyeing me from under a disheveled mop of hair, one hand conspicuously lingering in the pocket of his sweatshirt. The expressions on the young men's faces range from frigid to glacial. I break my eyes away and continue walking. A subtle shuffling indicates that I won't be alone.

They've just got somewhere to go this direction. Nothing to worry about.

A bus rumbles past but doesn't slow. A single old man is staring into the night from the illuminated interior, lost in a daydream or his own reflection. I'm nearly at the corner and, other than my skulking shadows, all pedestrians seem to have evaporated. *Isn't this supposed to be the city that never sleeps?*

I'm just considering breaking into a run when a smoke-black

Cadillac materializes from the side street. It oozes to the curb at the corner ahead of me and, as I approach, hearty chuckles trickle from the darkness of the open rear window. "Benjamin, Benjamin, Benjamin. We've been looking all over for you. You had us worried, my friend."

The door swings open and the dome light illuminates the plush interior and the lounging figure of a substantial, well-dressed man in his forties. His glossy hair matches his Burt Reynolds mustache. I've never seen him before. "You shouldn't just go wandering off around here, Ben. The locals can get territorial in the wee hours."

I stoop to peer into the car. The driver is a hulk in a suit coat. The man in the back pats the seat next to him. "Get in."

"I don't know you."

The man's eyes narrow, but then his face lightens and he gives me a cheek-stretching grin. "I forget how young you still are, Ben. Of course! This is your first time meeting me." He extends a hand. "Gioachino Amadeus. But call me Geo." I let his hand linger in midair. Finally, he pats the seat next to him. "Come on. We'll get you out of here."

I glance back down the sidewalk. My flock of followers has stalled out mid-block and is idling near a barred grocer's shop. A few of them are involved in subtle conversation, but the tall one is still just staring at me.

"How did you know where to find me?"

Geo stretches his arm along the back of the seat with a knowing smile. "We time travelers have to stick together, Benjamin."

"Mym sent you?"

"You don't think she'd just leave you out here on your own do you? You can trust me, Ben. We're destined to be great friends."

"Most of my friends drive themselves."

"Well then, it looks like you're moving up in the world. Now hop in. We've got places to be."

I take one last look at the city skyline, blending vaguely into a motor oil sky, and climb in. The Cadillac ebbs back into the street, and as the dome light fades, we are swallowed by the ocean of night.

Continue the adventure now! You'll find The Chronothon available here.

books2read.com/u/4AgO1o

ALSO BY NATHAN VAN COOPS

In Times Like These

The Chronothon

The Day After Never

The Warp Clock

Clockwise & Gone

Other Series

Sword Fight: Kingdom of Engines

Faster Than Falling: The Skylighter Adventures

IN TIMES LIKE THESE RECAP

Previously, In Times Like These

Benjamin Travers has been electrocuted. What's worse, he and his friends just woke up in the 1980s. With little money and no idea how they've gotten there, the friends seek out Robbie's grandfather; a widower they know does not have long to live.
Investigation into their predicament reveals they aren't the only persons displaced in time. A dangerous killer also shares their fate. The friends gain help from Malcolm Longines, the sleuthing assistant to renowned scientist Dr. Harold Quickly. They learn the deadly consequences of toying with time when Malcolm discovers the remains of others who didn't survive the journey.
Dr. Quickly trains the five friends to jump through time, using watch-like chronometers, and anchors in specific places and times. After a training mishap, Ben finds himself confronted by Elton Stenger, the killer from their own time. The near-deadly encounter at a gas station forces the friends to decide whether to deal with him and risk their own return home, or flee to the future. Ben is caught between his best friend Blake's obses-

sion to get home to his girlfriend, and Robbie's desire to save his grandfather.

    Things get more complicated for Ben with the arrival of Dr. Quickly's worldly, time-traveling daughter, Mym. Sensing she knows more about their future together than she is letting on, Ben is eager to know her better. Robbie's grandfather's stroke sends the group to the hospital where they witness a newscast showing the lab on fire. Ben and Carson race back in time to retrieve items vital for their trip home, and encounter Stenger inside the lab. Ben opts to flee the scene and rejoin his friends. With Dr. Quickly and Mym's disappearance, the group is on their own. Robbie and Carson stay behind, intending to catch up later, while Ben, Francesca and Blake make for home.

    The plan derails in Boston when the trio realizes they are missing an important tool for getting back. Seeking out "Guy Friday," a drunken time traveler from the future listed in Dr. Quickly's journal, the three hope for help, but are left worse off when Guy and his brother rob them of a chronometer.

    A photo from Montana leads the three to a younger Mym, and Cowboy Bob, her burly companion. Hitching a ride to 2009 in Bob's hot air balloon, the three return home, but while Blake proposes to his girlfriend, Francesca and Ben realize they've got the wrong timeline, a timeline where they never left. Scrambling to find their mistake, Blake considers offing his duplicate self to be with the woman he loves, while Ben struggles with guilt upon learning that Carson has died, a victim of the killer he failed to deal with.

    Determined to right the wrongs, the three return to the eighties, but the plan to stop Stenger fails. Blake gets shot and Francesca is taken hostage. Desperate to find her, Ben searches the lab, but instead discovers Malcolm bound and gagged. Before Malcolm can warn him, Ben triggers an incendiary device, trapping the pair and forcing Ben to once again flee using time travel.

Alone in the desert and fearing he has condemned his friends to a fiery grave, Ben struggles to face his failures. Encountering an older version of himself in the desert, Ben trains to defeat his fears and master his time traveling skills.

With new confidence in his abilities, Ben plunges back into the lab and finds Francesca. Tackling Stenger out a third floor window, the climactic fight ends at high speed on the freeway, when Ben knocks the villain into traffic.

The reappearance of Dr. Quickly means the group can finally return home, but once there, Ben is not eager to go back to his old life. Luckily Mym has other plans and invites him to join her for more time traveling adventures.

ABOUT THE AUTHOR

Nathan Van Coops lives in St. Petersburg, Florida on a diet comprised mainly of tacos. When not tinkering on old airplanes, he writes heroic adventure stories that explore imaginative new worlds. He is the author of *In Times Like These*, *The Skylighter Adventures*, and a new alternate history series, *Kingdom of Engines*. Learn more at www.nathanvancoops.com

Copyright © 2020 by Nathan Van Coops

All rights reserved.

No part of this book may be reproduced in any form or by any electronic or mechanical means, including information storage and retrieval systems, without written permission from the author, except for the use of brief quotations in a book review.

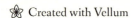 Created with Vellum

Made in the USA
Monee, IL
11 February 2022